A SKY FULL OF SONG

A SKY FULL OF SONG

SUSAN LYNN MEYER

union
square
kids

NEW YORK

Union Square & Co., LLC, is a subsidiary of Sterling Publishing Co., Inc.

Text © 2023 Susan Lynn Meyer
Cover illustration © 2023 Union Square & Co., LLC.

ISBN 978-1-4549-4784-4

Library of Congress Cataloging-in-Publication Data

Names: Meyer, Susan, 1960- author.
Title: A sky full of song / Susan Lynn Meyer.
Description: New York : Union Square Kids, 2023. | Audience: Ages 8 to 12. |
    Audience: Grades 4-6. | Summary: In 1905 North Dakota, eleven-year-old Russian
    immigrant Shoshana is bullied for being Jewish, but after listening to the music of
    her homeland, she is reminded of the resilience and traditions her people have
    brought all the way to the prairie.
Identifiers: LCCN 2022037178 (print) | LCCN 2022037179 (ebook) |
    ISBN 9781454947844 (hardcover) | ISBN 9781454947868 (trade paperback) |
    ISBN 9781454947851 (epub)
Subjects: CYAC: Farm life—Fiction. | Schools—Fiction. | Bullies and bullying—
    Fiction. | Music—Fiction. | Jews—United States—Fiction. | Ukrainian
    Americans—Fiction. | North Dakota—History—20th century—Fiction. | BISAC:
    JUVENILE FICTION / Family / Siblings | JUVENILE FICTION / Social
    Themes / Religion & Faith | LCGFT: Historical fiction. | Novels.
Classification: LCC PZ7.M571752 Sl 2023 (print) | LCC PZ7.M571752 (ebook) |
    DDC [Fic]—dc23
LC record available at https://lccn.loc.gov/2022037178
LC ebook record available at https://lccn.loc.gov/2022037179

For information about custom editions, special sales, and premium purchases, please
contact specialsales@unionsquareandco.com.

Printed in the United States of America

Lot #:
2   4   6   8   10   9   7   5   3   1

02/23

unionsquareandco.com

Interior design by Liam Donnelly
Title page background: Yugoro/iStock/Getty Images Plus
Crane illustrations and title type: Ramona Kaulitzki

For Ken

One

1905

At first, they only threw tomatoes. Then it was rocks. Soon you couldn't tell what was the splatter of tomato and what was blood. Women screamed and ran, stumbling over rolling cabbages, crashing into tipped-over carts. Others frantically tried to snatch up squashes and radishes and onions before they were trampled.

"Tsivia!" Mama shouted. "Perle!" She grabbed my little sisters, pulling her shawl over their heads, as if that could protect them.

"Libke!" I ran to my older sister, who stood frozen behind our potato cart. Something struck my cheek. Tomato splattered all over me. Drunken peasants laughed.

"Come on, Libke!" I screamed. "Forget the potatoes!"

I had to yank her arm to get her to run. But then she moved fast. A rock whistled by my ear as I knelt near Mama. "Let's go! We're all here!"

"I can't run with two babies!"

"I'll take Pearlie! Give Tsivia to Libke!"

Mama grabbed the heavy market basket, heaped with cabbages and onions.

"Leave it!" I wanted to shout, but it was our food for next week. And we'd already lost the cart and the potatoes.

Pearlie wailed, and I pressed her curly head against my shoulder. Mama and Libke and I hurried as fast as we could while lugging toddlers and a heavy basket, trying not to slip on the smashed bits of vegetables. The attackers were behind us now. Ahead of us in the fleeing crowd, old Faivish hobbled unsteadily with a cane and a sack of last winter's apples slung over his shoulder.

Suddenly two of the tsar's soldiers—Cossacks with huge mustaches—were blocking the road.

"You here, with the slow ones! Are you a man or an old woman?" one of them taunted Faivish. The Cossack grabbed Faivish's cane. The other kicked him. Faivish fell. The apples rolled away.

Faivish pushed himself up and screamed at the big soldier with the mustache. Blood came out of his mouth when he yelled, along with a bit of tooth. "Coward!"

His daughter wailed, kneeling by him.

"Jew parasites!" The soldier struck madly at the crowd. He caught the side of Mama's leg, and she went down, striking her head on a rock.

"Mama! *Mamenyu!*" Libke and I cried out together.

"Get the little ones to safety," Mama whispered, as Libke wiped blood out of her eyes. "Go!"

We didn't listen. Between us, we pulled Mama to her feet, leaving the fallen basket and our cabbages rolling in the dust.

Somehow, with Mama drooping and limping between us, we got home. With less to eat than we'd started out with.

That night I lay in bed beside Libke, not sleeping, wishing desperately for Papa and our big brother, Anshel. They'd been gone so long. When the rumors started up about young Jewish boys being forced into the tsar's army again, Papa and Anshel had rushed to leave for America. Papa had always wanted to farm his own land. He'd heard of a family from a nearby village who had gone to America to do just that. So Papa and Anshel had headed to the same place. Now they were working hard, farming the rocky soil, Papa wrote, making a start for all of us. Papa said that it was our job, Libke's and mine, to help Mama and to get ready for America by studying English with Hirsh, the rabbi's nephew. I liked learning English well enough. It was fun to call my little sister Perle "Pearlie," because one day Hirsh had told me that would be her English name. But—America?

I understood why Papa and Anshel had to leave, of course. But now it almost felt as if they had disappeared from the world. We were all alone here, me and Libke and Mama and the babies, with Papa and Anshel all the way across the ocean in America. My belly felt hollowed out and cold, remembering how far away they were. So far away, I couldn't even imagine it.

Our cat, Ganef, snuggled between me and my sister on top of the red-and-blue crocheted blanket. Shivering, I stroked her, and she stretched her tawny foreleg out lazily.

Ganef was a peaceable sort of cat. Not the sort to fight unless she had to. Still, I ran my finger over the soft, pale-pink underside of her forepaw, feeling the tips of the claws tucked inside. Those knife-sharp edges made me feel just the tiniest bit safer.

I closed my eyes against the moonlight. The reassuring vibration of Ganef's purr rumbled against me, gradually making me feel less alone.

For the next few weeks, Malke, our kind next-door neighbor, helped us tend to Mama. She brought us mushroom barley soup and potato soup and, once, on Shabbos, a whole roast chicken. She insisted on doing part of the wash, the very worst part. Soon the twins' diapers were waving merrily in the wind every afternoon behind her cottage.

"People will say I've had a baby!" she giggled to Mama. "From their mouth to God's ears! How are you feeling today?"

Mama smiled back faintly. "Still dizzy. Can you write a letter for me?"

I was in the other room, washing dishes. Ganef rubbed against my ankles, and I handed her a bit of fish from one of the plates. I could have written a letter for Mama, I thought. But I guess she wanted a grown-up to do it.

"To Shmuel?"

"Yo." Mama nodded, then winced. "I keep forgetting to hold my head still. Please tell Shmuel . . ."

She lowered her voice, but in our small cottage I still heard every word. "Tell him it is getting too dangerous here. Attacks on Jews are happening more and more often. Tell him, even if he has to borrow, he should send the tickets as soon as possible. It's time for us to leave Liubashevka and join him and Anshel in America. In Nordakota, America."

Two

I was angry with Mama nearly the whole voyage to America. Except when I was too seasick in the stinking steerage quarters to do anything but hold my belly and moan.

It had taken Papa nearly another year after Mama's letter to scrape together enough money for our steamer tickets. I heard Mama whispering to our neighbor Malke that he had also sent money for an exit permit and bribes for the Russian border guards. When the tickets and the money came, Mama counted it over and over, into the night. It wasn't yet enough, Libke and I knew. So Mama busied herself selling whatever she could to raise money for our travel to Hamburg, where we would board the ship. Then we packed. We could take only our most important things, Mama said.

But Mama and I didn't agree on what was important.

"The samovar?" I wailed, watching her take apart the precious brass tea urn and nestle the pieces into a trunk. "Pillows and feather beds? Those take up much more room than Ganef would!"

"We're leaving all the animals behind, Shoshana," Mama said wearily. "You know I've sold the cows and the poultry. We can't take animals on a steamer to America!"

"Ganef isn't just another animal! She's part of the family. We've raised her ever since she was a kitten!"

"Shoshi and I would take care of Ganef the whole way, Mama," Libke said softly. "You wouldn't have to do anything."

"You know the saying for something impossible, girls," Mama had said, trying to make us laugh. "'*Vi kumt di kats ibern vaser?*' And the Atlantic Ocean is a very big *vaser!*"

"'How are you going to get the cat across the water?' doesn't mean something impossible, Mama," I insisted. "It means something difficult."

"I already have four daughters to keep track of, plus all our baggage, on a long journey to a new country," Mama had said firmly. "More difficult, that I don't need."

"Little sisters are a lot more difficult than a cat," I muttered to Libke later. "Mama didn't say we had to leave *them* behind!"

"Oh, Shoshi, you don't mean that!" Libke had whispered, tucking her arm through mine. "Ganef will be fine here with our neighbors. Malke promised she'd take very good care of her."

But I wouldn't be fine without Ganef. Being on the ship now, after the struggle and worry of getting our family out of the Russian Empire and across Germany to the port, was a relief, but it also gave me time to worry about my cat. Even weeks and weeks after I'd kissed her goodbye for the last time, my eyes still leaked tears whenever I thought of her.

Other people had brought animals on board the ship. A wiry German man and boy had the cutest small, spotted dog with them. The boy was always running after him, calling, "Schnitzel, Schnitzel! Come back!" So why couldn't we have brought our cat?

I clutched the railing, looking out at the blue-gray waves. Cold sea air rushed against my face. We were nearly in America now, people were saying, even though no land was yet in sight. The ship would dock by afternoon, they said. Soon we would be in America.

Would Ganef truly be safe, living with Malke and Dov in Liubashevka? I knew that Malke, who now had diapers from her own little boy—sweet, apple-cheeked Josef—whitening in the sunshine behind her house, would take good care of her. But a few months after the peasants and the Cossacks, the cruelest of the tsar's soldiers, had smashed up our market, word came that there had been a pogrom in the next village. The following morning, I saw a wailing cat with a burned tail streaking down the deserted road in front of our house. I shuddered, remembering those cries. After what had happened to Mama, I'd kept Ganef inside, though she complained miserably at first. Malke had promised she would keep her inside too. But what if one night Dov shoved Ganef outdoors and those drunken Cossacks came back to our village?

In Nordakota, where Papa and Anshel were struggling to farm the rugged land, there were no Cossacks. Papa had said so in his last letter. Papa said America was a safe place for Jews.

And for their cats. I thought that last bit, though. It wasn't in his letter.

"You're thinking about Ganef again, aren't you, Shoshi?" Libke was standing in front of me, windblown and panting, the twins pulling on her. "Remember how much Malke loved her? Don't worry! Ganef is probably plump and happy right now, purring on Malke's lap."

"Baby Josef is probably on Malke's lap," I said to my sister, sniffing and smiling a little. "Even Malke wouldn't hold a cat instead of her own baby!"

"Well, then, Ganef's probably on her own cozy blanket in front of the fire, rolling onto her back and stretching out, meowing the way she does. Come on, Shoshi, play with me and the little ones. We'll need to go back down to steerage soon."

A little hand tugged on my skirt, and Pearlie looked up at me. "Shoshana is sad?" she asked worriedly, putting a little hand in mine. "Shoshana wants Ganef?"

I swiped my eyes with my other hand and bent down to tickle Pearlie, who was tugging on my sleeve now. "I'm fine. I'm going to catch you two!" I warned them in the scary goblin voice they both loved. Pearlie and Tsivia shrieked in delight and ran a few feet away, then stood grinning back at me. I chased them, bent over and growling, until we were all warm and panting, and my heart didn't ache quite so much anymore.

A few hours later, we were all waiting on the ship's deck in the harbor. Everyone had crowded to the railings to see the Statue of Liberty, weeping with joy, as the ship steamed past. But by now the mood had shifted. Many of the passengers were sitting wearily on trunks and suitcases. We could see America. New York, America. But we weren't getting any closer.

Near us, a group of men grumbled. A woman hushed a crying baby.

We watched at the railing with our luggage around us. Two smaller boats took passengers away from the ship toward land. First the first-class passengers, then the second-class passengers. How much longer until our turn came?

A big American boy with an old tweed cap perched atop his dirty blond hair shoved in front of me, blocking my view. I drew in my breath to complain. Mama sternly put her finger to her lips. I scowled, wanting to push him away. But I didn't.

The boy glanced at us with an odd smirk. "Clarence!" he shouted into the crowd. "Over here!" Then he shoved himself back from the railing. I couldn't back away quickly enough. He slammed into me, stomping on my toes, and ran off.

"Are you all right, Shoshana?" Libke asked.

I wiggled my foot. It was sore, but it didn't hurt more when I moved it. "I think so. He was so rude! He did that on purpose."

"People are just getting impatient." Mama sounded tired.

I grabbed the railing and faced the wind again. It whipped bits of my wild, curly hair around my face. Next to me, Mama leaned forward too, and the wind tugged at the soft *shtern-tikhl* covering her hair. Pearlie butted against Mama, moaning.

"Why ship not going?" Tsivia whined.

Mama patted their heads. "We have to be patient, girls. Libke, Shoshana, can you try to entertain the little ones?"

"*Bahelterlekh!*" I announced. Tsivia let out a cry of delight.

"Not hide-and-seek in this crowd!" Mama snapped. "Think before you speak, Shoshana! I don't want to lose one of you right before we get there!"

"You just said to entertain them!"

"Not by losing them!"

"Everyone's here, Mama," Libke said soothingly. "And so are all our things."

Mama counted the bags for the hundredth time. "Three small bundles. One large one. The trunk. Tsivia. Perle. Libke. Shoshana." She smiled wearily. "Four girls. Five pieces of luggage. Nothing lost yet!"

"I'm sure they'll let us go to land soon, Mama," Libke said. "Then we just have to find the train to Nordakota."

"Not yet!" exclaimed Mama's new friend Frayda, who was from Ukraine like us. Frayda was sitting on a trunk, bouncing her baby grandson. "First we go to the Ellis Island for lots of checking," she said. She nuzzled the baby's belly and he giggled.

"Checking?" Mama asked.

"Doctors. Checking to be sure no sickness is coming into the country."

"But we were already examined in Germany! Before boarding the ship!" Mama looked nervously at Tsivia, who had been feverish early in the voyage. She cupped her pale cheek.

"Just pinch a bit to make them pink when the time comes," Mama's friend said reassuringly, squeezing her grandson's cheek softly between her thumb and forefinger. "*Nu*, the little one is better now. About that you don't need to worry."

Pearlie gazed thoughtfully at Mama's friend. Then she reached out and pinched Tsivia's cheek with her fingernails. Tsivia screamed.

"No, Pearlie!" Libke scolded.

"Hush now, Tsivia," Mama scooped up Tsivia. "Hush, *mamele*."

Mama's friend tssked sympathetically and walked off, singing to her grandson.

Pearlie looked confused. "I pinched like the lady says!"

"Not now," I told her. "She meant Mama would do it later. And gently!"

Suddenly someone rammed me from behind. My teeth closed on my lip. I stumbled into Libke and Pearlie, and we all fell against the railing. Pearlie wailed. I grabbed her to me, tasting the sharp tang of blood.

Leering at us was the tweed-cap boy from before—and another one, even bigger.

"Careful!" Mama rebuked them sharply in Yiddish, tightening her hold on Tsivia.

But they just smirked. Suddenly, one of them grabbed the edge of Mama's *shtern-tikhl* and yanked. Hairpins scattered. Mama's hair tumbled down around her face. "*Rag head!*" he jeered. He whirled Mama's headscarf around, whooping, and hurled it into the ocean. Mama gasped. She clutched at Tsivia with one arm and reached for the wounded spot on her head with her free hand. In the place where her head had hit the rock after the Cossack struck her, there was a bare patch of shriveled, pink skin where her hair had never grown back.

The boys ran off, shoving their way through the crowd. "*Rag head!*" they jeered again as they ran, pointing back at Mama. People turned and stared. The word *head* I knew. It meant *kop*. But what did *rag* mean?

Whatever it was, I knew it was cruel.

"This is America!" the bigger boy jeered.

Mama's cheeks flamed with humiliation. She threw her shawl around Pearlie and Tsivia, pulling them against her the same way she had that day in the marketplace.

It wasn't right! We had come here to escape all that. We were going to start a new life here. A new life working the land, Papa had said proudly.

But those mean boys were sneering at us from across the deck. And in the harbor, in front of us, Mama's best cream-colored headscarf bobbed, sinking slowly.

Three

Once we got into the huge building on Ellis Island, I wondered why we'd been in such a hurry to get there. Clamor slammed into us. While we waited in the crowd, Libke helped Mama twist her hair back up and tie the apron she was wearing over the coils. Mama's two other scarves were tucked away deep in the luggage. Mama's apron was pretty, embroidered with large pink roses, but to me it still looked like an apron. It was strange seeing Mama with an apron on her head. I peeked around, embarrassed. Was anyone noticing? What would people think?

An hour went by, and then another. Hordes of people were crammed together in vast, echoing spaces, everyone hot and uncomfortable, even with the soaring ceilings. Everyone cranky and smelling bad. Everyone bumping into one another with suitcases, everyone shouting in different languages. Babies cried. Small children whined, especially my little sisters.

We waited in line after line. At the end of the longest was a man who looked like a soldier, but I guess he was a doctor. His lip curled as he examined people quickly, one after another.

14

After each one, even after our elegant, fastidious Mama, he wiped his hands back and forth on his sharply creased pants. My face burned, watching him do that.

The worst thing, when it was my turn, was the eyes. He grabbed each of my eyelids, one after another, and flipped them inside out. It felt so creepy, I nearly gagged.

But then it was over. We were off the island. We were in the city, with Frayda and her husband and daughter and grandson, finding our way to the train station together. Frayda's train came almost right away. She kissed Mama goodbye.

"*Zayt gezunt un shtark.* Be healthy and strong," she almost sobbed out, and then she hurried off, catching up with her husband and daughter, lifting the baby out of her daughter's arms and fussing with his blanket, dabbing it against her eyes.

We sat on a long wooden bench to wait. Mama got out herring and *sukhares*.

"Here, children," she said, handing us each a piece of the dried bread and a bit of herring. "Eat!"

Tsivia leaned sleepily against Libke.

"Story?" she asked.

"Once there was a little white goat with brown feet," Libke began.

Pearlie snuggled against Libke on the other side. "Brown feet goat is a naughty goat?" she asked eagerly.

"Oh, yes," said Libke. "The naughty goat was named Malgrim, and he was always getting into trouble. One day, Malgrim was very, very hungry . . ."

Mama rested her head against the bench back and closed her eyes.

I took a nibble of my dried bread and herring. "I'm going to walk around and look at the station, Mama, all right?"

"All right, Shoshana," Mama said. "Don't go far. Be back in plenty of time for the train."

Before Mama could change her mind, I snatched up the bundle of pillows I'd been carrying and hurried off.

By the time I was halfway across the vast room, I realized I could have left the pillow bundle behind. The pillows weren't heavy, just awkward. I adjusted them under my arm, broke the dried bread in half and smashed the herring in between, licked my fingers, and pushed it into my pocket. I could eat later.

I followed the crowd heading for a pair of double glass doors. Weary-looking people hurried by, some of them rushing into the station and others rushing out. Some lugged straw suitcases, belted closed. Others had cardboard cases. Some heaved trunks and cloth bundles like ours. One tall girl balanced a large palm-leaf fan atop a wobbly stack of paper-wrapped parcels.

Just inside the doors, a man stood behind a pushcart full of small American flags. He held one up and waved it, calling out. I wished I could buy one for my sisters, but I didn't have any money. I let the crowd carry me through the propped-open doors.

Outside, street noises hit me. Shouts, cries, the clopping of horses, the wheels of wagons. And the smells! Many different foods at once, smoke, manure, the smell of crowds of people, and beneath it, through it all, the lurking smell of garbage.

I worked my way to a quiet spot near the train station wall and gazed about. Streets illuminated by lamps. So many people going about their business as if it were daytime. And beyond the people, such tall buildings. Weren't the people afraid, living up so high?

I felt dizzy, confused, and exhilarated, all at the same time. The city pulsed with energy. I felt it racing through me.

All at once, a boy yelled, a dog snarled, and something rushed toward me, brushing my ankles. I looked down. A scrawny black-and-white kitten cowered under my skirt. A hairy dog came to a stop, barking ferociously. Beside me, half-hidden by my skirt, the kitten arched its small back and hissed.

I couldn't help laughing at the courage of the tiny creature.

A boy pushed through the crowd and yanked the dog's collar. "No, Bruno!" he scolded. "Sorry." He touched his cap, pulled Bruno away, and disappeared into the crowd.

That boy seemed to think the kitten was mine. I squatted down to examine her. The kitten backed against the wall and looked at me warily, hunching against the dirty white stone. She was obviously a stray. She was thin, terribly thin, with patchy fur. I held out my fingers, crooning. After a few moments, she crept forward and sniffed. Then I felt a tiny, rough tongue against my fingertips. I laughed quietly. She must be tasting the remnants of herring.

"Are you hungry, *ketsl*?" I murmured.

She meowed.

I had some herring in my pocket, and I wasn't *that* hungry. Well, I *was* hungry, but I wasn't starving. The kitten was. Moving slowly, trying not to startle her, I drew out the bread and herring, mashed the fish to a soft paste, and held it out. "More fish, *ketsele*?" I murmured. "It's all right. You're safe!"

She was an American cat, but she seemed to understand my Yiddish. Hesitantly, she crept toward my hand and devoured the food.

I watched her tiny, flicking pink tongue, so careful, so neat. When she had finished the fish and licked my fingers clean, I tried stroking her, slowly and gently, on the top of her head. After a little while, I slid my fingers around behind her head and gently rubbed below her ear. She nudged back against my hand, and I felt the rumbling of a purr.

I don't know how long I stayed there, stroking her, as people rushed by. Long enough to need to shift from one foot to another, as my knees began to ache, and then to adjust my thick gray skirt under me and sit down, gently, slowly, cross-legged on the New York sidewalk.

"Here, *ketsele*," I murmured, patting my lap. She looked up at me with green-gold eyes and meowed plaintively. "No need to be scared. Come."

She hesitated and then, in a single neat little jump, she leaped onto my lap and settled there, warm and soft and impossibly light and small. My heart melted. How could this tiny kitten stay alive here, where she might starve or be crushed by wagon wheels or hurrying feet or be attacked by slobbering dogs?

I started to hum a Yiddish lullaby, one Mama sometimes sang when she was putting Tsivia and Pearlie to sleep. When I got to the end of the song, I started. How much time had gone by? I needed to get back to Mama and the others.

But I couldn't leave this kitten behind. I just couldn't. She might die.

All at once, I made up my mind. "You are going to be my cat," I said firmly. "And you are coming to Nordakota with me."

I pulled the pillow bundle close to her and opened it. "In you go," I crooned, gently slipping my hand under her and sliding her in. She trod a circle on the top pillow and settled down. I petted her gently to calm her, then tied the bundle loosely to keep her in but to let air in too. Then, carrying the bundle gently in front of me, I went back into the station.

Four

I didn't want to join the others until the very last minute. That way there would be less time for them to notice anything. I wandered around, crooning to the kitten, pretending I didn't see Mama gesturing for me to come over.

"Your name is Zissel," I murmured to her, peeking in and touching her cool nose. "Because you're so sweet."

By the time the train station clock struck quarter past the hour, Zissel was snoring softly inside the bundle. I tightened the knot and hurried back to the others.

"Didn't you see me waving at you?" Mama scolded. "I thought I was going to have to send Libke over."

The train pulled up with a great hiss of steam. Tsivia was nearly asleep, so Libke carried her up the steps onto the train. Mama spread her shawl on the floor in front of her seat for Tsivia and Pearlie.

"Get a *kishn* out of your bundle for them, Shoshana," Mama said.

I jumped up, reached into the bundle on the rack overhead, and slipped out the bottom pillow. Zissel lifted her head inquiringly, but settled back down. I tied the bundle up again, being sure to leave enough air for her to breathe.

"The *kishn* is smelly like fish!" Tsivia moaned.

"Nice soft pillow," I told Tsivia, patting it. "Pearlie, put your head on it too."

It probably smelled like something worse than fish, and it was my fault. Zissel had probably peed on it! But smelly *kishn* or not, Tsivia and Pearlie both slept soundly.

I couldn't, thinking about Zissel overhead. The train jolted and whistled, waking me every time I drifted into sleep. The jostling banged my head against the seat back and the window. Outside, through blurry eyes, I saw vast, dark nothingness. From time to time we sped past a cluster of lights and then on into mile after mile of empty darkness.

At the Chicago station the next day, we changed trains, leaving our big bags with a porter. I clutched my bundle tightly as Pearlie hopped along next to me. It wriggled, and Zissel made a small, angry sound.

"Ganef?" said Pearlie hopefully, looking around.

"Ganef's back home with Malke, remember?" Libke told Pearlie gently. "She didn't want to come to America."

"How do you know, Libke?" I scowled. "She did too, Pearlie, but Mama wouldn't let us bring her!"

Libke shook her head at me. "We all had to leave things we loved behind," she said quietly. I knew she was thinking of her two best friends, Rivka and Bela. Libke had always tried to include me when they came over to drink tea. But they were older, and I had never wanted to sit around the way the three of them did, talking and working together on feather beds or embroidery. Now Libke sighed, and I slipped my arm through hers and squeezed.

"You two keep an eye on the little ones," Mama said. "I'm going to step out to look for a peddler."

"Why?" I asked excitedly. "What are you going to buy?" I was *so* tired of dried bread and herring.

"Fruit, if I can find any. But you girls stay right here. Libke, take these." She handed Libke a few coins. "In case of emergency. Or in case a fruit peddler walks by while you are waiting for me."

I relaxed a little. For a while, I wouldn't have to worry about her noticing Zissel.

Pearlie tugged on my skirt. "Shoshi, I need to pee!" she whispered loudly.

"Tsivia? You too?" I asked.

Tsivia shook her head and chewed her fingernail.

"Now!" Pearlie demanded.

I grabbed her small, sticky hand, the bundle with Zissel under my other arm, and we raced for the washroom, zigzagging through a crowd of tired-looking people lugging bundles and straw suitcases. One stout man tenderly carried a large birdcage with a parakeet inside. As we passed him, I heard Zissel mew again, angrily this time, and the bundle lurched and squirmed.

I'd only been inside a washroom like it once, at the steamer station in Hamburg. Sinks with metal faucets where you only had to turn the handle to have water come out, hot or cold, whatever you wanted. And a line of doors, with spaces under them.

I reached for one. But it wouldn't budge. There was something on it I'd never seen before. A brass plate with a coin slot. All the stalls were the same.

The washroom door swung open, and Libke and Tsivia came running in behind us.

"Tsivia changed her mind," Libke panted. "She needs the washroom too!"

"We can't get in!" I said, pointed at the brass plates. "They're locked!"

Pearlie hopped from foot to foot, moaning. "I need to pee!"

"We have to put in a coin," I said. "Let's see which one fits. Hurry!"

Libke hesitated. "Mama said it was only for food or emergencies."

"It *is* an emergency! They're about to wet themselves!"

Libke held out a handful of coins. I grabbed one that looked the right size and slid it in. The handle turned and I yanked open the door.

"Go!" I told Pearlie, holding the door so we wouldn't have to put in more coins.

"Hold me!" she wailed. I steadied her and then Tsivia.

"My turn," said Libke. I turned my back to give her privacy.

"You take the little ones out and see if Mama is back," I said, still holding the door. "So she can go too, without us paying more money. I'll wait."

I set my bundle down to hold the door ever-so-slightly ajar as I sat. Fancy, I thought. Nothing like our outhouse at home.

But I shouldn't have let my mind wander for even a moment. My bundle gave a great lurch, and an angry black-and-white kitten shot out and slipped under the divider into the next stall.

Five

"Zissel!" I pleaded. "Come back!"

I crouched in front of the toilet. Through the crack underneath the stall divider, I saw two black forefeet, two white hind feet, and a lashing black-and-white tail. Zissel hissed.

I heard the washroom door open. "Mama's back. She doesn't need to go," Libke called. "She says hurry. The train leaves soon. She bought us orange fruit. They smell so good!"

"Libke!" I came out of the stall. "I need more money!"

"More? Why?"

"It's important!"

I pried her fingers open, grabbed another coin, shoved it into the slot, and opened the next door. Zissel was perched atop the high toilet tank, glaring. Behind me, Libke gasped. "A cat? Shoshana!"

"Good kitty!" I murmured. "Good Zissel!" I slowly stretched out my hands. Zissel yowled. Just as my fingers were about to touch her, she leapt off the toilet tank and slipped back through the crack into the stall we had just come from. It had locked behind me.

"I need another coin, Libke!" I demanded. "Please!"

"We can't! We only have a little! Mama was worried when I told her we had to pay for even one toilet!"

"But Libke!" I wailed. "She's my new kitten! I found her in New York!"

"You know we can't keep her!"

I fell onto my hands and knees on the cool tile and reached under the stall blindly. Heat streaked across my hand. "Ow! She scratched me! It would be faster if you just gave me a coin!" I shouted.

"I can't!"

I wasn't going to leave little Zissel behind. I bit my lip. The tile floor was dirty. But I had no choice. I tucked my hair inside the back collar of my dress, got down onto my belly, and wriggled into the locked stall.

Zissel backed up, hissing, and before I could corner her, she slid back under the way she had come.

I squirmed back out, feet first, my dress sliding up over my knees.

"You're going to be so filthy!" moaned my sister.

Zissel mattered more than being clean. I dove back under the next door. Zissel stood on the toilet tank, hissing.

"Shh, Zissel, shh!" I murmured. I held up my left hand, wiggling the fingers. She turned her head to follow the movement with her eyes. When her head was turned, I darted out my right hand and seized her from behind by the scruff of the neck. She went quiet in my hands then, as if I were her mama cat. Murmuring gentle words, I wriggled back out, feeling my dress sliding up again.

"Got her!"

"Shoshi! Mama's going to be so mad! She said no traveling with cats!"

"She said she didn't want to travel with a cat *to* America. She didn't say we couldn't travel *with* a cat in America!"

"You know what she meant! You know she'll say no!"

"So don't tell her! Just untie my bundle, quick! You don't have to do anything else."

Libke hesitated. Then she knelt and undid the knot. I cuddled Zissel, purring words of comfort, tucked her back inside, and we ran out into the station to join the others on the platform.

Mama had each of the twins securely by the hand. "Oh, Shoshana! Your hair!" she lamented. "Couldn't you tidy up a bit in the washroom?"

I shoved it back from my face. With a rumbling so loud it made the ground tremble, steaming and whistling, the train rushed toward us. Tsivia screamed and ducked her head into Mama's skirt.

"We're going to get in so much trouble!" Libke whispered.

I squeezed Libke's hand. She was such a good sister. She hadn't said, "*You* are going to get into trouble." She had said, "*we*." Libke hated doing anything Mama said not to do. But she was helping me anyway.

Libke was better at being sneaky than I expected. The train ride seemed to last forever, even though the thick-skinned orange fruit Mama had bought was absolutely delicious. Whenever she doled them out, I peeled and ate mine slowly, licking up every drop of the juice. The tangy smell lingered afterwards, sweetening the stale air.

I watched the bundle in the rack overhead. Luckily, Zissel seemed to be exhausted from her life on the streets and willing to sleep on a cozy, warm pillow most of the time. Whenever the bundle started to heave, I looked at Libke desperately. Each time, Libke quickly convinced Mama and the twins to walk to the observation car at the end of the train with her. When they were gone, I let Zissel out. I tied my pink hair ribbon around Zissel's neck, holding one end so she couldn't run off, cleaned out any mess she had left in the bundle as best I could with scraps of newspaper, and fed her and gave her water from the bottle Mama had packed for us.

Once, a lady walked by, saw me playing with Zissel on the floor in front of our seat, and frowned. A little boy a few seats away watched me eagerly and always talked excitedly to his mother when I got Zissel down. None of the passengers nearby seemed to speak Yiddish, though, so nobody told Mama.

Every time Libke pulled open the door to the train car as she came back with Mama and our little sisters, she said something loudly so I could hear them coming. Once they nearly caught me. Pearlie raced through the jolting corridor and hugged my leg just as I was shoving Zissel's bundle back into the rack.

"I saw rabbit outside!" she shouted.

"Ooh, lucky!" I said, making rabbit ears at her with my fingers. "Was the rabbit hopping?"

Pearlie made rabbit ears back at me and giggled, jumping in the aisle like a rambunctious baby bunny. As the others slid back into the red velvet seats, I eyed the bundle worriedly. But the rumbling and rocking of the moving train had lulled Zissel right back to sleep.

My stomach got jittery on the last day, as the conductor called stops in Nordakota. If I hadn't had Zissel with me, desperately needing her freedom, I would almost have wanted to go on riding the train forever, to have stayed in this strange world that wasn't anyplace, just the space in between.

"We're getting close now," Mama said. "Tidy yourselves in the washroom. Especially you, Shoshana. I don't know how you manage to get so messy! We want to look nice for Papa."

Libke and I washed the babies' faces and hands and sent them back to Mama. Libke turned her back, and I retied the blue hair ribbon she always wore, adjusting the ends on which she had embroidered tiny white flowers, making sure that they hung perfectly evenly against her honey-colored hair.

Then Libke helped me dab at the worst smudges on my dress and work a comb through my grimy, snarled curls. "Is Zissel all right?" she asked.

"Yes. She needs to get out, though. Maybe Mama won't care that I brought her once we're there. Maybe I can pretend that I found her in Nordakota." My voice trembled a little. Would Mama be really mad at me? Would Papa?

"Do you remember Papa and Anshel?" I asked Libke, suddenly feeling panicked. The train lurched, and the comb caught on a snarl. "Ouch!"

"Stand still! Of course I do." But Libke sounded less sure than her words.

"I *am* standing still! It's the train that's jostling. Remind me of something about them! Quick!"

Libke gently teased at a snarl at the bottom of a lock of my hair. "Well, of course you remember Papa, so big and laughing, playing with us. Lifting you up on his shoulders and galloping around outside? And you remember that game we used to play with Anshel, the Rabbi Hillel game?"

I smiled. Yes, that I remembered. Anshel had invented the game. It came from the story about Rabbi Hillel being taunted by a fool, "Tell me what is in the Torah while standing on one foot."

I picked up a foot and wobbled so much I bumped into one of the walls of the washroom. "Don't try it on a moving train, Shoshi!" Libke moaned. "Or I'll end up accidentally ripping all your hair out!"

Rabbi Hillel stood on one foot and told the fool, "What is hateful to you, do not do to your fellow man." That was the core of Jewish belief, Papa had told us many times.

So Anshel and Libke and I competed to see who could say those words the most times in a row while standing on one foot. We got really fast at rattling out, "What-is-hateful-to-you-do-not-do-to-your-fellow-man, What-is-hateful-to-you-do-not-do-to-your-fellow-man," over and over again.

"You got up to twenty-one once," I said. "You were the champion!"

"Not twenty-one. Twenty-three! And I could have done a lot more. Anshel was so mad, because he had only done nineteen! So he pushed me over. There, your hair's good enough. You'll remember everything when we see them again, I promise."

Pearlie leaned her weight across my leg when I slid back into the seat. "Papa is nice?"

"Of course he's nice," I assured her. "He's our father!"

Even Mama kept nervously smoothing her skirt and adjusting the flowered apron on her head. It still looked awkward and bunchy to me, like an apron, not a *shtern-tikhl*. Why did Mama have to tie a cloth over her head anyway? Here in America, most ladies didn't seem to. Instead, Mama could arrange her hair carefully, so the scarred spot wouldn't show, and wear an American hat. If Mama hadn't been wearing a *shtern-tikhl* on the ship, those boys wouldn't have bothered us.

The train screeched and hissed to a stop. "Shakton!" called the conductor.

We clambered out of the train and looked about, bewildered. The day was ending. A few dark buildings rose nearby, but beyond them the prairie spread out, as vast and undulating as the sea. I heard a shout. A big man and a tall, lanky boy ran along the platform toward us.

"Family! My family!" Papa's voice broke. He caught us all up into a huge hug. "At last. You're here!"

Six

Afterwards, though, it seemed as if none of us knew quite what to say. Papa's wagon, pulled by two snorting oxen, jolted slowly over a rutted path through mile after mile of empty, rolling land. Mama perched between him and Anshel on the bench in front. Libke and I snuggled down in the straw in the wagon bed, leaning against the side, with Pearlie asleep in front of me and Tsivia asleep on Libke's lap. I kept one hand on Zissel, who was snoring softly inside the pillow bundle, and watched Mama's figure, silhouetted, dark and upright, against the fiery glow of the sunset.

From time to time, Papa said something I couldn't hear, and Mama murmured back.

Papa looked different. I hardly recognized him now, with his long, shaggy beard and hair. Anshel was different too. How had our mischievous, reedy older brother become as tall as a man, with a dark shadow on his upper lip?

Beside the wagon, shadows lengthened. A whirr of insects rose from the tall, murmuring grasses. The sky flamed over the vast, flat land, the colors changing as I watched. Maroon, violet, slashes of gold, a wide wash of shimmering silver fading into auburn. A single star hung overhead. The great loneliness brought tears into my eyes. The colors swam together. The sky glowed a fainter orange and yellow and crimson, like dimming embers, and then, as I watched, the sun slid down below the glowing rim of the earth. As it disappeared, coolness rose from the ground. The smell of damp earth filled the air. The insect sounds grew louder. I shivered, pulling my shawl tightly around myself, and leaned against Libke. She put her arm around my shoulder.

Anshel struck a match and lit a lantern. He held it steady between his feet. It cast a pale gleam onto the dark grasses ahead. The wagon jolted on and on through the thickening darkness, into what seemed like the very end of the world.

I must have slept, because the stopping of the wagon awakened me. I grabbed for my pillow bundle with Zissel inside and climbed out of the wagon behind Libke. Papa and Anshel lifted the trunk and the large bundles. Mama helped the little ones down. They stood sleepily, clinging to her.

The pale lantern light fell on what looked like a small, shaggy hill, a swelling upward of the earth. Then I saw a pipe sticking up, and a door and a window sunk deeply into the front.

"Home!" said Papa proudly, in his deep, hoarse voice. "Anshel and I built this *dugout* ourselves."

Anshel glanced over at me and Libke, from where he was tending to the oxen. He looked awkward but proud. I didn't know the funny English word Papa used. I'd never seen such a house. No words came into my head to answer with.

"*Nu!*" said Mama faintly, lifting up Tsivia. "All by yourselves!" She followed Papa down the steps.

Pearlie let go of Mama's skirt and looked back at me. "Shoshi!" she said plaintively, reaching out her hand.

I took her little hand in mine. "Come. You can go to bed inside."

"No!" Pearlie wailed. "Not want to go in hole!"

"It's not a regular hole," I told her. "There's a secret house inside. Don't you want to see?"

"House?"

"Yes! See the door?"

"Carry me!"

I hefted her up to my hip and lugged her and the bundle down the stairs and into the cold underground darkness. It smelled like roots and earth.

"Dark!" Pearlie wailed again, as I tried to put her down.

The lantern swung in Papa's hand, casting moving shadows. He proudly showed Mama a big iron bed against one wall, the tin stove with a pipe going up through the cave roof, and a table and benches beside the bare, dark window.

As he was showing us the shelf he had made, hung on the wall above the table, Anshel came in with a heaping armful of hay.

"It's for the girls to sleep on," Anshel explained to Mama shyly. "It's not a bed, but it's dry and warm."

"*A dank*, Anshel." Mama patted his arm. "We'll make a pallet for the girls. Should they sleep on this side of the hut?"

Papa's lips tightened.

Mama's face got blotchy red. "I mean, what did you call it, the house? The 'duck-out?'"

"Dugout," said Papa. "This is how everyone starts out living here, on the prairie. Did you see lots of forests as we came? What about you, girls?" Papa sounded as if he were trying to make a joke but not quite managing. "Wood is very scarce here, very expensive. Lumber has to be brought in by railway."

I realized Papa was right. We had seen almost no trees. I thought with a pang of the silvery white birches behind our house in Ukraine. Sometimes, back at home, when Mama had scolded, I would slip out of our house at night, lean my cheek against cool bark, and listen to their leaves rustling. I loved those trees, and I'd forgotten to tell them goodbye.

"I'm very sorry, Shmuel," Mama murmured. "I truly meant no harm. I just didn't remember the American word. *Dug out*." She uttered the syllables carefully. "Dug out. Now where will my Anshel sleep?"

She looked at our brother fondly. He drew a hay-stuffed pallet made from feed sacks out from under the bed and showed it to her.

"So, girls, you sleep here, against this wall," Mama said. "This is good."

Anshel spread out hay, going back to bring in more armfuls from the barn until we had a thick layer. Libke and I untied the biggest bundle and spread out a blanket on top of it, and then the feather beds. I put a pillow at one end for the little ones, and one at the other end for Libke and me to share. Mama undid the twins' boots and tucked our little sisters under another blanket. Tsivia had never really woken up. Pearlie went right to sleep, sucking her thumb.

Mama had made Papa feel bad, I knew. But she had done it without meaning to. She just hadn't remembered the English word. The rabbi's nephew had never taught us that one. *Dugout*. It *was* like a hut or a cave, this small, dark, strange room.

Mama hadn't seen our Papa in three years, since he and Anshel came here to Nordakota, America, at the end of the world. What if they didn't like each other anymore?

Papa made a fire in the stove. I kept peeking at him, trying to turn him back into the Papa I remembered. He couldn't be taller, surely, but he seemed so. When he stood, his head almost brushed the earthen ceiling. His shoulders were wider than they used to be. I was sure about that.

I crouched with Libke and Anshel in front of the fire. The cold of the ground crept up through my skirt, and I reached my hands out to the flames, watching the reflection dance on my fingernails. Papa offered Mama a sack stuffed with beans, maybe, or potatoes, and she sat down on it carefully, her back very straight. Papa settled onto one himself.

"So this is America," he told us. His voice echoed around the room. "What do you think? A country where there is land even for strangers like us, if we are willing to work it. Even for Jews."

"Free land," murmured Mama. "It's remarkable, Shmuel."

"Well, not quite free. We have to '*prove it up.*'" Papa said the English words proudly.

"What does that mean?" Mama asked.

"We have to build fences, acre after acre of them," Anshel explained. "You couldn't see, in the dark."

"And till the soil, to grow food to live on. And build a home," Papa said, stressing the last word a bit.

"It's a very good home, you know," Anshel muttered to me and Libke. "The first months here, we camped in the wagon under a canvas roof. In wind, rain, everything. With wolves howling outside." He imitated the howl of a wolf. "And we had hardly anything to eat. You think this is living rough?" He sounded irritated, but what had *we* done? "This is luxury!"

I shivered. "Thanks for bringing in the hay for us," I said. Papa and Anshel must have been so cold. So alone. So afraid. Was this the same mischievous big brother who used to be the best at finding mushrooms when we were hunting them in the forest? Who knew the names of all the birds and could explain all the differences between them? Who used to play the Rabbi Hillel game with us and splash me in the stream? He was seventeen now, with a face like a grown-up man's.

"And we must pay a claim fee, and taxes, of course," Papa explained. "They're not so cheap. And we must live here, not in town."

I didn't remember Papa's voice being so loud. Maybe it had turned that way because every day for the last three years he and Anshel had needed to shout out "*Hineyni*! I am here!" against all that emptiness.

"Doesn't anybody else live nearby, Papa?" I asked shyly.

"Other farmers have claims. But each claim is 160 acres. So everyone is spread out."

The fire crackled and snapped. I heard a rustle behind us. Zissel must be getting hungry and thirsty again. I wouldn't be able to keep her hidden much longer. We just needed to get through the night, and then tomorrow I would pretend I had found her outside on the prairie.

"The girls must be tired," Papa said. "Bed?"

We splashed water on ourselves quickly from a bucket in the corner. Soon Libke and I were lying together at one end of the pallet, with Pearlie and Tsivia at the other end. The hay was crackly and it prickled, but under the blankets with my sisters I was already warm and cozy. I lay on Pearlie's side, and Libke had crept in next to Tsivia. I hoped Pearlie wouldn't wet the bed in the night. She still did sometimes, especially when she was scared.

Anshel lay on his pallet across the room with a blanket and pillow, and Mama climbed into the big iron bed, waiting for

Papa. Papa lowered the lamp and puffed it out. The bedstead creaked as he got in next to Mama.

I reached across my little sisters for Libke's hand, and she stretched her arm out to me, clasping my hand tightly. Outside the dugout, wind wailed over miles and miles of emptiness. Something howled. A wolf? I shifted uneasily. A dry, skittering noise, like wind rattling a seedpod, came from somewhere closer by. It was so cold here, so strange being under the ground. Suddenly I felt a desperate yearning to be back home, back in the bed where Libke and I always slept with Ganef between us, under the familiar red-and-blue crocheted blanket, surrounded by everything we'd known all our lives. Tears came into my eyes, and, even crowded with my sisters, I felt terribly forlorn and alone.

Anshel turned over, sighing. His pallet rustled, and I remembered Zissel.

I pinched my leg to keep awake. When I heard heavy, slow breathing from Papa and Mama and Anshel, I would tiptoe over to Zissel's bundle and give her water.

Anshel and Papa dropped into sleep right away, I could hear it. Then I heard Mama's whistling, sleeping breath. Libke's hand softened in mine, so I could tell she was sleeping too.

Outside, an owl's long hoot trickled down the sky. Then again. And again. A faraway, lonesome sound.

Ten, nine, eight, I counted slowly in my head. Zissel must be starving. At zero, I would tiptoe over and care for my kitten.

And suddenly a yowl came from across the room, followed by a sharp, angry mew.

Libke startled awake.

Mama sat up in bed. "Eh?" she asked, confused.

"What's that?" Papa's voice thundered, cloudy with sleep. "What made that noise?"

"Nothing, Papa," I whispered.

"That wasn't nothing!" Papa's voice boomed. "There's a cat in here! All this way, across the ocean, you brought Ganef?"

My heart ached when Papa said Ganef's name. Was Malke taking good care of my cat?

"No, no!" Mama protested. "The girls did want to bring Ganef. But I told them it was too difficult."

The bed creaked. Papa thrust a stick into the embers. With a pop, light flared up from the kerosene lamp. Papa's face, above it, was shadowy and strange.

"Girls?" he demanded.

Moving stiffly, I got up from the pallet. Libke got up behind me. My stocking feet were numb on the cold dirt floor.

"I found a stray kitten in New York," I said, hanging my head. "I knew Mama wouldn't want me to bring her. But I did. She needed me!" I looked up at my parents. "Her name is Zissel."

"You brought her all this way? Without me seeing? But how?" Mama gasped.

I pulled the now wriggling and howling bundle out of our heap of belongings and unknotted it. Zissel leapt out. I took out the stoppered bottle of water.

41

"I put her into my bundle," I whispered. "I gave her water and bits of my herring. Mine only, Mama! I took her out when you were in the observation car." Mama drew in her breath.

"Daughters!" Papa sounded stunned.

"It was me, not Libke," I said. "Libke didn't even know about the cat at first. Not until Zissel escaped in a train station washroom. Then Libke only helped because I begged her to."

I poured water into my cupped hand, squatted, and held it out to Zissel. She lapped it up. Then she calmly began to lick herself clean, not minding all the eyes on her, right in the middle of the earthen floor.

I stood up and looked at Mama, who sat looking confused in the rumpled bed. "I'm very sorry I disobeyed, Mama," I said. "But I just couldn't leave her all alone to die! A cat needs a family too. I just couldn't!"

"I did help to hide the cat, Papa, Mama," Libke said, her voice trembling. "I'm sorry too. Truly, it wasn't all Shoshana's fault."

Papa stared at Zissel as if Libke hadn't spoken. "A cat!" he bellowed.

"Why that Papa man is shouting?" Pearlie complained sleepily, sitting up. Tsivia whimpered.

Papa crouched down by the kitten. She was washing her ears now. He cupped his big hand very gently over her tiny head. Then an odd sound came out of his throat.

He was laughing! Papa was laughing! He stood and looked down at us. His eyes were bright and kind, just the way they used to be.

"You brought a kitten here," Papa cried joyfully. "Here, where there isn't a cat to be had for love or money, not for miles and miles around. Here where the mice and rats are taking over! Where they are so bold, they run about even in the daytime. You brought a kitten all this long way, hidden in a bundle, on the railroad! Thank you, daughters! *A groysn dank!*"

Papa reached his strong, warm arms around us. "Of course, you should always do what your Mama tells you. But this time, only this one time, Shoshana," he held me off and looked at me sternly, "it is good that you did not. We won't need to feed this new little family member for long. As she grows, she'll find all the mice she can eat here."

He looked at Mama and smiled. She smiled back, including all of us in the warmth of their new togetherness.

"What a blessed day!" Papa said. "At last, we're together again, all seven of us! And, thanks to these willful daughters of mine, we have a new cat. A precious cat to keep our home snug and comfortable! Even here. Even on this Nordakota prairie."

Seven

I woke up late, feeling a purr vibrating through me. At first, I couldn't remember where I was, or why it was a tiny black-and-white creature, not Ganef, beside me in the bed. Then I saw the dark walls and low ceiling, and Mama stirring a pot atop the stove. I pushed the blanket aside, and brushed bits of earth that had fallen during the night from my face and hair.

"Ah!" Mama said, smiling. "You must have been tired."

"Good morning, Mama. Where are the others?"

"Papa and Anshel are tending to the animals. Here's a bit of fish you can give Zissel."

"Thank you, Mama!" I hugged her and squatted by Zissel. "Where's Libke?" I asked

"Libke took the little ones out to look around."

I shoved my feet into my boots and ran to the door. "Come, Zissel!" I called.

"Only for a moment!" Mama cried. "Call the others in for breakfast."

The light outside dazzled me, coming at me from all sides, making bright pinpricks swim in front of my eyes. As my vision cleared, I saw a vivid blue sky stretching out all around, over wire fences and huge mounds of rocks in one direction, and beyond them shorn fields and stacks of wheat. Around and beyond the fields were endless reaches of waving brown and gray grasses. The prairie smelled dry and sweet in the October sun. Insects sang wildly. I had never seen such an enormous sky, more powerful and tremendous even than the land, deep with clouds, dizzyingly vast. From somewhere nearby, a bird rose into the blue, uttering a series of sharp cries.

The world felt brand-new. Like the very first morning of creation. So different from the bleak, lonely grayness of last night. Not the end, but the very beginning of the world.

"Shoshana!" Libke and the little ones raced toward me, their hair blown about as they ran. Papa and Anshel emerged from another structure, larger than the dugout. Anshel lugged a heavy bucket.

I ran over to them with Zissel bounding along beside me. "Breakfast, Mama says," I called.

Papa nodded. "We'll just check the chicken coop first. Take the milk in, Anshel. Come this way, Shoshana. It's on this side of the barn. Are you good with chickens? You remember what I taught you and Libke about gathering eggs?"

I looked at Papa blankly. He expected me to remember something he'd said so long ago, before he left for America? "I don't like chickens," I admitted. "Libke always did it."

"*Shah*," Papa tssked, and I felt my face getting hot. "You'll need to help out with all the chores here. No shirking! *Nu*, I'll remind you. The Torah says we should always be kind to animals. We drive poultry away before taking their eggs so that they don't see us doing it and feel sad."

Or feel like pecking us either, I thought. "I'm sure Libke did it that way. She does everything right. And Papa, I didn't shirk! I did lots and lots back home! I took much more care of the twins than Libke did, especially Pearlie, and she's the hard one. Tsivia always does what she's told. Well, nearly always."

Papa ruffled my hair. "I'm sure you did. Go ahead, now. Drive the hens off and look for eggs. No need to be frightened."

I was glad Papa only had two hens. I took a deep breath and waved my hands at them. "Go, go!" I shouted.

Complaining, the hens fluttered down from their nest and stalked off on scaly feet toward the open barn door. I shuddered.

"Now check the corners of the nesting boxes," Papa said. "Reach in your hand. Anything?"

I rummaged around the smelly place, which was much bigger than two chickens needed. "Did you used to have more hens?" I asked.

"We lost three last winter. And one of these two doesn't lay so well. Anything?"

My fingers closed on something round and warm. "Found one!"

"Good," said Papa. "Not so bad, was it?"

I shrugged. It wasn't great. I still didn't like chickens. But Papa was smiling at me.

We walked back to the house side by side. I matched my step to his long strides and took deep breaths of the sweet prairie air. Zissel pounced joyfully around in the grass. When we went back into the dugout, I couldn't see at first. It was so dark after the outside brightness.

Mama had made *kulesha* with the cornmeal, and she was happy to have the egg to add to it. Anshel's bucket held new milk from the cow. One after another, we poured the milk over our mush. I slowly stirred the creaminess and took a big, delicious, warm spoonful. A clod of dirt fell onto the table. I jumped back as a spider scuttled toward me. Anshel smirked, brushed it away, and shoveled another spoonful of *kulesha* into his mouth.

"First things first," Mama said to me and Libke, when Papa and Anshel had gone back to the fields. "Washing. We'll take baths, and then we'll wash the clothes. It'll feel so good to be clean!"

Libke and I lugged buckets of water from the stream nearby. Mama heated it in a gigantic pot over the stove and poured it into a tin tub she set in the middle of the dirt floor.

We bathed the babies first, watching them laugh and splash. I was next, then Libke, then Mama. Mama had kept a pot of warm, clean water on the stove. We used it to pour over each other's heads, scrubbing and then rinsing out the soap. Then we combed each other's hair outside in the sun. After all those days of being itchy and dirty and greasy, the bath made me feel light and free. Libke ran the wide-toothed comb gently through my curls, easing out the tangles. I closed my eyes, breathing in the scent of the dry grasses, feeling almost as if I were made of sun and wind, like the air around us.

Mama took the fine-toothed comb and carefully examined each of our scalps, and then Libke did Mama's. "No nits on any of us!" Mama exclaimed, astonished. "What a miracle that is—not a single *layznisl*, after all those days on that filthy ship."

"No nits on me!" Pearlie shouted. "No nits on Tsivia! No nits on Shoshi!"

I dumped the bathwater, trying not to splash Pearlie, who was running in circles around me and Zissel, who kept darting underfoot. Zissel nosed curiously around the puddle. That wasn't like Ganef! Ganef had always hated water.

Then Libke took one bucket and I took the other, and we ran to the stream to fetch water to wash the clothes. We did that several times, wearing only our last clean shifts. Mama said that the men were far off in the fields and that we were miles away from anyone. And it was true. All we saw, as we ran through the grasses to the stream and lugged the buckets slowly back, were jackrabbits bounding up ahead of us, and here and there, curious small underground creatures that poked their heads up out of the earth and peered at us with bright eyes.

We took turns sloshing the clothes around in a gigantic pot hung over a fire outside, filled with bubbling, soapy water.

The water got grayer and grayer. We lifted out the heavy, wet clothes, rinsed them in fresh water, and laid them out to dry on the grass. Overhead, clouds blew swiftly across the never-ending sky.

Mama set a pan full of water on the cookstove and started chopping potatoes from one of the sacks.

"Papa says there are pickles in the root cellar under the barn," she told me. "Go fetch us one for supper. Just one, because we need to save most of them for winter, when there's nothing else green to eat."

"But my dress is still drying. Should I go just wearing my shift?"

"Papa and Anshel are still off in the fields. It's all right."

"I'll come with you," Libke said. "Anshel showed me where the root cellar is this morning, before you woke up. A Scotsman lived here before them, Mr. McIvor. He dug it before he gave up on his claim."

"Where did Papa get the pickles from? Did he and Anshel make them?" I asked, as I followed her into the lean-to on the side of the barn.

"Anshel said that they were a gift from a lady here, Mrs. Kantor, on the High Holidays. The Kantors are our *landslayt*—neighbors from back home! They're how Mama and Papa knew to come to Nordakota, remember? The village they come from is only half a day's walk from Liubashevka. Now all the Jews for miles around drive their wagons to the Kantor homestead for Rosh Hashanah and Yom Kippur. The Kantors have a big barn, big enough for everyone to stay. Mrs. Kantor felt sorry for Papa and Anshel, men all alone cooking and farming, both. So Anshel said he and Papa came home the day after Yom Kippur with two big barrels of pickles. Delicious ones!"

I was glad Libke was with me, going down the steps into the dark cave under the barn. Roots dangled from above, catching in my hair. I fished inside the murky barrel with a long metal fork, trying to spear a pickle.

"They're so slippery," I said, annoyed.

"Let me try," she said. "You have to be patient. Oops! It got away. Just one more minute, Shoshana."

I fidgeted, eager to get out of there. As soon as Libke plunked a pickle into the bowl, I ran up the sagging wooden steps into the fresh air.

By suppertime, we had clean, dry dresses to change into. Mama had a clean *shtern-tikhl* instead of the apron, and she had started a fire in the stove. We were all shy at supper. I listened to the crackling flames and the sounds of spoons against bowls. Mama's potato soup was delicious. I ate slowly as I came to the bottom of my bowl, stretching it out. I could happily have eaten another whole serving.

"There's a bit more soup," Mama said as Papa finished his bowl. "More for you, Shmuel? Anshel? A growing boy needs plenty of food. *Es gezunterheyt*—eat in good health! Tsivia, *mamele*, more soup? Are you still hungry?"

Tsivia shook her head. I dropped my spoon with a clang. Why didn't Mama ever call me *mamele*? Why didn't she ever ask *me* if I wanted more? My arms ached from all the buckets of water I had carried, all the scrubbing I had done, all the heavy, wet cloth I had wrung out. So what if Anshel was a growing boy? I was a growing girl, and I had worked hard all day too. So had Libke.

Anshel accepted the last of the soup and dunked his bread into it, slopping soup over the edge. I stared at him, horrified. Mama would never let Libke and me eat with bad manners. But she just smiled. Because he was a boy, I supposed. He scooped up a big spoonful of soup. A clod of earth fell into my bowl.

"Euh!" I exclaimed. "Mama, look!"

"That's life in a dugout, daughters," Papa said. "It's good, clean dirt. The same soil the food grew in."

We weren't supposed to *eat* the dirt!

"Papa," I asked, pushing my bowl away, "Did anyone live before you and Anshel on this land right here? It seems so lonesome."

"Nobody's farmed it much. McIvor had the claim first," Papa said. "But he moved on. He didn't 'prove up.' Before him, there were Indians. The Dakota. But there are none living here now."

"Why not?" I asked.

Papa sighed. "It's not a pretty story," he said. "With all the settlers moving in, there wasn't so much land for hunting anymore, and the Dakota were starving. The government made treaties with them, took their land, but didn't pay up. Then there was a big war about fifty years ago. Many Dakota were killed in the war or afterwards. Or starved."

The shadows of the flames in the stove danced on the walls and the dark, earthen ceiling. Papa got up and poked at the fire.

"But why couldn't they have land sections too, like us, Papa?" I asked.

A spark flew out of the stove, and Papa set his heavy boot on it, smothering it. He stretched, groaned, and sat back down.

"All this land here used to be Dakota land, you see. The United States wanted it for settlers. The Americans didn't believe Indians were civilized because they looked different, because they weren't Christian, because they lived a different way. They wanted to get rid of them."

"But why?" I wanted to cry out. "Why, Papa?" But I couldn't speak. I knew by now that there didn't need to be any other reason. Being different was enough reason to be turned on, to be driven away.

"So where did they go, the Dakota people?" Libke asked after a moment, and I could tell she was feeling the way I was feeling.

"North, I think," Papa said. "And west."

"I learned in school that they live on reservation land now. At Devil's Lake and Fort Berthold," Anshel added, tipping his bowl to get out the last bit of his extra soup. "Not such good land, probably."

"Instead of where they lived before?" I asked. "The way Jews in the whole Russian Empire had to leave their homes and move into the Pale?"

Across the table from me, Mama blanched. "You know about that, Shoshana? How?"

"I listen when grown-ups are talking, Mama!" I said impatiently. "Why do parents always think kids don't hear? But, anyway, isn't it the same thing?"

Outside, the wind howled, gusting into the chimney pipe, making the fire flicker.

Papa's face was somber as he nodded. "*Yo*, it *is* the same sort of thing. Different country, different people, but . . . yes, they were forced out of their homes. Driven away."

"At least the government gave them land, Anshel said," Mama added.

"It's not fair," I said furiously. "That's not 'giving' them anything. It's not right."

Papa rubbed the back of his neck with both hands, as if it ached. "No," he said. "It isn't right."

"Sometimes the plow turns up an arrowhead," Anshel said. "And every now and then we see a few Dakota people in town. They make beautiful beadwork. Sometimes we see women selling beaded clothes, bags, pincushions. Things like that."

Everyone was quiet.

Because they were different, I thought. Driven away. It made me feel sick.

I looked at my family finishing their meal, their shadows flickering against the wall as the flames danced. Before we lived here, had a Dakota family lived in this very spot? Maybe there had been a girl my age. Had she had a brother or sisters? What kinds of games did she play with them? What kinds of chores had she done? Did she like cats, like me? My family was able to be here now because she and her family had been forced to leave.

I shivered. It wasn't right. It wasn't fair.

"Mama," I murmured, as we washed the dishes after the meal. "Couldn't we stretch something under the ceiling to keep dirt and spiders from falling on us?"

Mama's face brightened. "Good idea," she said. "We could use sheets. But we don't have many extra. Maybe Papa has some burlap."

Papa said we could use some feed sacks he had in the barn. But when Mama asked about whitewashing the inside of the dugout to make the house clean and bright, he shook his head.

"I just don't think we can afford the lime, Mirele," he said regretfully. "We have debts to pay back. We must be very frugal. Anshel and I have managed fine without whitewash."

After supper, I followed Anshel out to the barn, warily, not sure if he might snap at me but eager to see the animals. Through the dusk a furry shape bounded toward my brother, wagging its tail. My wariness about Anshel evaporated.

"We have a dog?" I cried, kneeling down. "Was she in the fields with you? What's her name?" The dog was already licking my hand.

"That's Berchik, Little Bear. He looks like one, don't you think? He's a boy dog."

"I like him! Where did he come from?"

Anshel knelt down beside me and ruffled Berchik's dark, furry head. "He just showed up one day. He was skinny and his fur was all patchy. He had a wounded foot. Papa made such a fuss over you bringing a kitten," Anshel said, rolling his eyes. "Well, *I'm* the one who noticed paw prints around the wagon one morning, smaller than wolf paw prints. And I'm the one who coaxed Berchik into trusting me. I'm the reason he stayed. When you and Libke and the babies were living with Mama, all snug and cozy in our home, Papa and I were shivering in the wagon under canvas, relying on Berchik to keep us safe."

"Hi, Berchik," I said, rubbing the dog's furry head, not sure why my brother was so cross all the time. Cozy? Liubashevka? I had loved our home in Ukraine too, and especially our trees, and Ganef, of course, but had he forgotten why we left? Had he forgotten the attacks on the Jews? The Cossacks, the blood-thirsty mobs, the burning of villages? I didn't like the thought of wolves, but pogroms were worse.

Berchik flopped down with a sigh and rolled onto his back. Tentatively at first, then more confidently, I stroked his belly. "Is Berchik's foot better now?" I asked.

"Yes," Anshel said. "You're all fine now, aren't you, Berchik?" Berchik heaved himself to his feet, and Anshel thumped Berchik's back harder than I would have. But Berchik whined and wagged his tail as if he liked it. Anshel scratched between his ears. "I washed Berchik's injured foot and bandaged it and now he's fine. *Hunky-dory*, that's what they say here."

My big brother might be cranky, but he knew how to do so many things, even talk like an American. The rabbi's nephew hadn't taught us that word. "*Hunky-dory*," I practiced under my breath, trying to say it the way Anshel did. Berchik was *hunky-dory* now. Zissel was *hunky-dory* too. Maybe Anshel knew the answer to a question that had been bothering me ever since our ship docked in New York.

"Do you know what *rag head* means, Anshel?" I asked.

"*Rag head*? Well, *head* means "*kop.*" *Rag* is "*shmate.*" I never heard *rag head*. Why?"

I shrugged. "No reason."

Anshel looked at me sharply, but he didn't ask any more questions.

"Doesn't Berchik sleep in the house?" I asked. "He wasn't there last night."

"He's a working dog, a guard dog. Sometimes he sleeps in the house, sometimes the barn. We let him decide. Anyway, you're lucky he didn't. He'd have sniffed out your kitten right away and blown your secret! Come on, Berchik." Anshel whistled and patted his leg. Berchik got up and agreeably followed us to the stable. It was made with bricks of sod, like the dugout, but bigger. Inside were stalls.

"A milk cow *and* two oxen?" I said admiringly. "Those are the ones that pulled Papa's wagon. They're ours? What are their names?"

"That's Royt," Anshel said, as I stroked the milk cow's dappled red-and-white flank. "She's a Dairy Shorthorn. Good-tempered. And she gives lots of milk! And these here are Cantor and Muley."

"Cantor? Like the man who sings in the shul?"

Anshel grinned. "It's a joke. He's short-winded. Farmers round here call that singing, when an ox does that. And Muley, he's the most stubborn ox you ever met. That's why he has that name."

"Hi Cantor! Hi Muley!" I stroked Cantor's nose. He was red-brown, with big soulful eyes. Muley didn't look as friendly. "I can't believe we have all these animals! And the hens outside!"

"We bought them with the loan. From the Jewish Agriculturalist Aid Society. We have to pay it back in two years." He pointed to a pile of empty sacks. "We can take these for the ceiling."

I examined them. "The threads aren't very tight," I said. "A white sheet would be nicer. Brighter. But we don't have any extra. And even burlap will keep a lot of the dirt from falling."

Anshel scoffed. "Girls are awfully fussy! Ooh! I'm a spider. Eeeee!" he wiggled his fingers near my face.

I stuck my tongue out. "Boys!" I retorted. "Perfectly happy to live in dirt!" If he wanted to eat muddy soup and have spiders in his hair, that was his business. I didn't, not when just a little bit of effort would fix it. I picked up the burlap bags and saw something behind them.

"*Nu*, what are those?" I asked excitedly. Behind the bags were a few old bricks and a stack of big sheets of paper with bright pictures. Each one had a roaring lion in the middle surrounded by a ring of flames. On either side, fine horses reared up, with fancy tassels on their heads. "Do you go to school here? Can you read English? What does that say?"

"I used to go in winter term. When Papa didn't need me. I had to leave last year to help run the farm."

"Did you like the school? Are the other kids nice? Are there any Dakota kids?"

Anshel shrugged. "It was school. Easier than the *kheyder* I went to back at home. No, no Dakota kids. Some of the kids are nice, some aren't. Like everywhere. The papers say 'circus.' The circus must have come through Shakton some years back. Those are the posters."

"I wish I could see it! Do you think it'll ever come again? Where did the posters come from?"

"They were here when Papa took over the land. Mr. McIvor left a lean-to with a root cellar under it and part of the stable. A few railroad ties too. Pretty, aren't they?" He held up a poster and admired it. A slant of low light fell across the lion's roaring mouth.

"So pretty! And look, Anshel, the backs are such a beautiful white! Let's bring these back to Mama too! Maybe we can use these to paper the dugout!"

Eight

The next day, while Papa and Anshel were out in the fields, I worked with Mama and Libke in the dugout. Libke cut the burlap bags open and flattened them with a heated iron. I stood on Mama and Papa's bed to nail one end of the pieces of burlap into the hard earthen ceiling. Then I dragged the wooden bench around the room to attach the other ends. When I had finished, we had a neatly covered, tan-colored ceiling. Already the room looked brighter.

Mama had been excited when I brought in the circus posters the night before. Now she was sifting mouse droppings out of the cornmeal Papa had stored in a sack.

"We need to store this grain in barrels," Mama said grimly. "Sacks are unacceptable when there are so many rodents around."

"I told you, Mama!" I cried. I seized Zissel, kissed her, and held her up to Mama's face. "I told you it was always good to have a cat!"

Mama grinned at me. "You did, Shoshi," she said. "Let's hope she grows fast and turns into a good mouser. Take that pestle and start grinding some of this cornmeal into flour. We need it as fine as possible."

When it was flour, Mama added sugar and salt. Then she ground some more.

"Go collect some dried manure for a fire, girls," she said. Libke and I wandered around gathering it. Pearlie and Tsivia played in front of the dugout. I picked the chips up with just the tips of my fingers and wiped my fingers on my apron afterwards, the way the doctor at Ellis Island had wiped his hands after examining us.

Mama stirred the flour mixture into clear water, while I smoothed the walls with an oval stone and Libke rubbed them down with a rag. We took turns stirring the flour mixture until our arms ached. After a long time, it was thick and almost clear and sticky.

"That's our paste, girls," Mama said. She dipped a cloth and painted the wall behind the bed with it, going from top to bottom. Then Libke and I took the first poster, held it out taut, and pressed it against the wall at the top. We smoothed it out from the middle. It was a little crooked, but it made a bright spot of white in the dugout. Then we did another, just below. By the time our arms were too sore to keep going, we had covered two walls in white paper.

Tsivia stuck her head inside. "Pretty, Mama!" she cried.

Pearlie followed her. "I hungry and thirsty!" she announced, sounding outraged.

Mama brought boiled potatoes and salt outside, and we ate on the grass in the sun. The wind never stopped, restlessly moving one way and then another. The sun beat down, warming my dark, thick curls. Tsivia leaned against me, and I stroked her cool, golden head. It never got hot in sunshine. The sun flashed off her light, silken strands. My dark hair soaked it up.

Pearlie butted against me from the other side and climbed onto my lap. "My Shoshi!" she shouted, trying to shove Tsivia away. "My big sister!"

I laughed. "I'm a big sister to both of you, silly!" I said affectionately, patting her dark, curly head, which felt hot like mine. Tsivia put her finger into her mouth and leaned back against me with a sigh.

The world of the prairie was so alive, alight, full of bird and animal sounds and dried-grass smells and breezes. Zissel raced around in the sunshine until she got tired, then crouched behind the tall grasses, popping up now and then to leap after passing insects. I wanted to stay outside, like Papa and Anshel, not go back into the quiet underground darkness. But now, with two white walls, the dugout was much brighter. I papered the last two walls with Libke while Mama carefully took apart a pale blue dress with pink flowers that was too small for Tsivia. She held it against the deeply set, grease-paper window, then went outside to sew.

By the time the sky began to darken, we had white walls and a burlap ceiling. Flowered curtains hung by the window. Libke opened the trunk and got out our mezuzah. I polished it with a rag. Libke swept, making the hard-packed floor as clean as an earthen floor could be.

My arms burned with weariness and my hands were red and sore. But I was happy.

"What do you think Papa will say?" I asked Mama and Libke, as we hurriedly made soup for supper. "It's beautiful now!"

"The curtain's so pretty, Mama," said Libke. "It makes the whole room cheerful."

"We'll be glad of the brightness when the dark days of winter come," Mama said.

When I heard Papa and Anshel outside, banging the dirt off their boots, and Berchik's eager bark, I grabbed the mezuzah and ran out.

"We need to put the mezuzah up first," I called. "And then, come in and see the house!"

Anshel fetched nails and a hammer. All of us stood around and watched while Papa attached the mezuzah to the wooden doorframe of the dugout.

"It's been so long since I put one of these up that I hardly remember the words," Papa said. "Not since before Anshel was born. More than seventeen years that is now!"

"*Likboa mezuzah*," Mama said.

"Oh, yes."

We said the mezuzah prayer together as the sunset flamed in the western sky. Now the dugout felt like a home, our home. It must be the first mezuzah anyone had ever put up in this place, on this stretch of the vast prairie that was now Papa's claim. Mr. McIvor wasn't Jewish, so he wouldn't have had one. Before that, the Dakota had lived here. And now, driven out, they lived on reservation land. I thought about the arrowheads Anshel had found in the fields. I shivered. Would that happen to us? Would this dugout crumble and the mezuzah fall to the ground, forgotten, for someone, long years from now, to find as they farmed the land again?

Mama reached up and touched the mezuzah as she went in, then kissed her fingers. Libke did the same. Then I lifted first Tsivia and then Pearlie. And then I took a deep breath, touched the familiar surface, silvery and cool, and brought my fingers to my lips. A warm feeling rushed over me, and suddenly I felt strong and calm, able to face this new life in this new, strange world. It might not be our home for always, but it was our home for now. Wherever we went, we would have a mezuzah, and the new place would be home. Without realizing it, I had missed that feeling in the long days of our journey. Touching the mezuzah, kissing my fingers, and walking inside to a place of safety, a place of peace.

Papa and Anshel followed me. "Surprise!" Libke and I called, as they came in.

Berchik flopped down by the hearth with a weary sigh. Zissel picked up her head and gazed at him warily. I pulled Zissel onto my lap, stroking her so she wouldn't be scared of him.

Papa ran his hand down the neatly papered white wall.

"*Nu!*" Papa said slowly. "It does look nice. *Heymish.* Homey. There's nothing quite like a woman's touch! And these are the posters from the stable? Clever. But how did you attach them to the walls?"

"I ground some cornmeal into flour and added sugar," Mama explained. "It makes a nice, strong paste. It should last."

"*Ach.*" Papa sucked in his breath, looking worried. "*Nu,* what women need is different from what men need," he said slowly. "But our grain must keep all seven of us fed through the winter. The winters here are hard," he told Mama.

"I did not use so very much, Shmuel," Mama said uneasily. "The walls are not so large."

"It looks good, Mama," Anshel said after a moment, in his new, deep voice. "Reminds me of Liubashevka."

The lamplight flickered on the white walls and the colors of the curtains. We quietly ate our soup. I still felt proud of our bright new home. But Papa's words kept going through my head. I held Zissel close and shivered. "The winters here are hard."

Nine

"Papa," I asked after supper the next night. "Do you still play your fiddle?"

"Ach!" Papa smiled at me. "I haven't thought about the fiddle in a long time. I played a little last winter. Farmers have more time then."

"Do you like being a farmer, Papa?" Libke asked. "More than selling cheese?"

"It's certainly backbreaking work on this rocky soil. Anshel can tell you. But here we can own land, if we can prove it up! I never want to hear again the false things the rest of the world says about Jews. That we live off the work of others. Buying and selling, not making. My whole life, since I first heard that as a boy, I wanted to work with my hands growing food out of my own land, to show people what a Jew can do. Eh, Anshel?"

"Selling cheese, back at home, you worked very hard too," Anshel said.

"Of course. But I want to show everyone what I can grow with my own two hands." Papa spread his fingers and looked at his calloused palms.

The fire crackled and glowed. Shadows danced on the freshly papered walls. I shaped shadow puppets with my hands for the little ones, making a dog, a flying bird. Tsivia and Pearlie laughed.

Zissel leapt off the bed and swatted at the shadows. Berchik heaved himself to his feet and trotted over too. "Good boy, Berchik," I said, holding him gently around his big, shaggy neck to keep him from getting too close to Zissel. "Anshel, will he hurt her, do you think?"

Anshel shrugged. "I doubt it. He's tired out."

I let go of Berchik, watching him closely. Zissel pounced, chasing after a shadow Pearlie was making for her, then stood, quivering, watching, as Pearlie held it still. Berchik sniffed the base of Zissel's tail. She startled and turned around. Warily, they sniffed noses. Then Berchik settled down with a sigh, and Zissel leapt onto Tsivia's lap.

"Good dog," said Tsivia. "Berchik is good dog. Not fighting."

"Zissel's good too," I said. "She didn't fight either."

Berchik thumped his tail against the earthen floor.

"Do you feel lonely here, Papa?" Libke asked. "With no neighbors nearby? No friends to talk to?"

From the corner where she was sitting, I heard Mama sigh softly. So Libke and Mama felt it too, how big and lonesome this land was. But it was also wild and free.

Papa nodded. "*Nu*, it's true that the farms are far apart. There's no one to play music with here, not often anyway. No Motke the baker with his clarinet. No Beinish playing his *tsimbl*. No weddings, no dancing. I'm out of practice."

"But I love it when you play by yourself!" I said. "Didn't you teach Anshel? You were starting to, before you left for America. Remember?"

Anshel shook his head. "When we got here, I was too tired."

Papa knelt by the iron bedstead and pulled out his battered fiddle case. When he opened it, the light of the fire gleamed on the warm brown of the fiddle, nestled on faded red velvet. I ran over to touch it, and Pearlie followed me.

"Bird?" Pearlie asked.

I don't know why she said that. "It's a fiddle, Pearlie. It makes beautiful music. Won't you play, Papa? Just one song?" I begged. "Pearlie has never heard it. Or maybe she has, when she was just born, but she doesn't remember."

Mama smiled. "I wonder if she does remember, somewhere in that clever head of hers! When I was expecting the twins and Papa played, I was sure they liked it. They always woke up inside me and kicked!"

Papa tightened the strings of the bow and ran rosin over it. He stood up, put the fiddle to his shoulder, and tuned it. "Hear that, little ones? Does it sound familiar?" He plucked a string, smiling at Tsivia, who ducked her head against Mama's side.

Berchik lifted his head. I sat down to listen, and Pearlie climbed onto my lap.

Papa played. The rich, full sound filled the air, first yearning, then merry, then soaring and haunting and yearning again. I closed my eyes, listening, and memories filled me. Home. The two-room cottage, where we'd lived our whole lives. White birch trees murmuring behind the house. Buttercups in the meadows, poppies in the garden. The sound of cocks crowing at sunrise. On Friday afternoons, carrying Mama's sweet golden challah, warm in the cloth, from the village oven. The light-brown water of the stream we waded in, the tiny fish nibbling at our toes. Dancing feet at weddings. Going outside to empty the slops after supper and stopping with cold, muddy feet to watch the last rosy light over the rooftops as the sun went down.

After Papa's bow went still, I opened my eyes, and that whole world faded away.

"So beautiful, Papa," I whispered. But it was also sad. Was that how he and Anshel had felt on the long, dark winter nights, with the wind prowling around the dugout, so far away from us?

Papa pulled me toward him and stroked my head. "And what did you think, small ones?" he asked Pearlie and Tsivia. "Do you remember? Do you like Papa's fiddle?"

Tsivia nodded solemnly. "I bemember."

Pearlie nodded too, and lifted her hands high over her head, craning her head back. "Papa's fiddle like a bird. Flying."

"I don't see how you could've been too tired to want to learn to play like that, Anshel!" I burst out. "I'd give anything to learn!"

Anshel frowned. "You don't know what it was like when we started here. You try learning the fiddle after digging up rocks all day. My fingers were stiff and blistered. All I wanted to do was sleep."

"Still . . ." I stroked the gleaming wood of Papa's fiddle.

Papa smiled. "You can try, Shoshana. You were too tiny before, but I think your hands are big enough now."

Papa rummaged in the case for a piece of chalk and made marks on the neck of the fiddle where my fingers would go. He showed me how to stand, resting it against my shoulder, and arranged the fingers of my left hand on the neck.

My fingers felt awkward, but my heart thudded with excitement. I drew the bow across the strings.

A sound somewhere between a screech and a scream came out of the violin. Tsivia yelped. Zissel leapt off her lap. Pearlie covered her ears.

"It takes time," Papa reassured me. "Try again. Draw the bow more lightly and a little faster."

I did. This time, Berchik howled, and trotted to the door. Anshel let him out and laughed, not in a nice way. "He can't stand it," Anshel said. My face went hot.

"We'll do more another evening," Papa said, patting my shoulder. "It takes lots of practice. *Yeder onheyb iz shver.* Beginnings are difficult, the way it says in the song you used to love, '*Oyfn Pripetshik.*'"

"Will you play us just one more tune first, Papa?"

"Yes," Anshel laughed. "To clear the sound of Shoshana's screeching out of our heads!"

I scowled at him and handed Papa the fiddle.

"Do you remember this one?" Papa asked. A lonely, haunting melody filled the small underground room.

I would play like that one day, I promised myself, as I lay on the pallet next to Libke, with Zissel curled between us.

The song "*Oyfn Pripetshik*" was right. Beginnings *were* hard. Because every beginning meant an ending too, the loss of whatever you had loved before. And even if there were bad things behind you, there was also always something that you had loved and lost.

Home felt impossibly far away now. We were here, in this strange, flat, bare new land. But the fiddle brought our old world into the new one, pulled the two together for a brief time while the sounds lingered in the air. Pearlie was right. The music of the fiddle *was* like a bird that could fly halfway across the world. Pearlie's little head was wise sometimes. I wondered what had made her think of birds. I wondered how she knew.

Ten

"Will we start school soon?" I asked the next morning.

I took a spoonful of golden *kulesha*, sweet with fresh milk from the cow, and savored it.

"Soon." Papa smiled. "As soon as Mama says so."

"Do any of the other kids speak Yiddish?" Libke asked.

"Yiddish!" Anshel's laugh had an edge to it. "No. There aren't any other Jews nearby. It's a tiny school."

"That's all right. Libke and me, we learned lots of English at home from Hirsh. And I've learned some new words already. *Hunky-dory, circus, washroom, dugout, prove up,* and *Dakota*!" I also knew *rag head*. But I didn't say that one.

"Listen to the child!" Papa smiled. "She has a *yidisher kop*! A good head on her shoulders!"

Pearlie banged her spoon. Cornmeal mush flew up into the air, and she laughed. Libke took the spoon away and wiped her face.

"Are there girls my age at the school? Can we go tomorrow?" I asked eagerly. Maybe I could find friends here, friends my age, the way Libke had had friends back at home. Good friends to laugh and tell secrets with, the way Libke used to with Bela and Rivka.

"Not just yet," Mama said. "Shmuel, our Libke and Shoshana need new dresses for school. Theirs are nearly rags now. Only good enough for chores. I'll make Anshel a new shirt too. Where can we buy some cloth?"

"In the town," Papa said. "There's a general store. I'll take the family on Thursday. Anshel and I can use a day off from mending fences. I need to buy some supplies. And the girls will need sunbonnets too, for walking to school. The sun here is fierce, even in the fall."

Papa stood up from the bench and scooped up Pearlie. "A family trip to town. What do you think, little ones?" Papa made her fly over his head, and she yelped with delight. He set her down gently and looked at Tsivia, who clutched Mama's leg and shook her head, her finger in her mouth. "If you're good," Papa said, "maybe I'll even buy you a bite of candy. What do you say?"

Tsivia peeked out at him. "Yes, Papa!"

"Us too?" I asked.

Papa laughed. "Of course. Even some for your beautiful Mama, if she likes!" He pulled her close to him and kissed her. Mama smiled and her cheeks went pink.

New dresses! Brand-new ones, not cut down. And candy!

The sun rose as we rumbled along the tracks to town. The wagon startled small birds from the grasses, and the wind blew restlessly, tossing wisps of our hair around our faces. A deer leapt up from shrubs by the side of the wagon tracks. The sun got brighter and brighter, and the shadow running along beside us darkened against the yellowing grass. It was warm and nearly noon by the time the tracks became a wider road. Papa pulled the oxen to a stop at a hitching post, and we all climbed down.

Ahead of us on a plank sidewalk, a storekeeper beat a small doormat into the dirt road. Two ladies wearing hats walked into a shop. I looked at Mama, tidily dressed but with a *shtern-tikhl* over her hair. I wondered if she felt bashful. After just a few days of only having open land all around us, as far as we could see, I felt awkward being among people again. And I wished Mama had a hat like the other ladies instead of a head-scarf. Her *shtern-tikhl* made us look so foreign.

Papa led the way to a large store with a striped awning.

"This is the general store," he said. "Come, Mirele. You pick out what you need. I'll do the talking for you."

The store was dim after the brightness outside. Papa and Anshel went to the back to look for tools and seed. Long shelves behind a counter held bolts of cloth. A thin woman with gray-streaked brown hair twisted up in a bun looked at us curiously. Near her, a girl about my age was sorting spools of thread. Her loose brown hair fell in curls over her shoulders, set off by two bright plaid ribbons that matched her dress.

So many colors and patterns of fabric! I'd never seen anything like it before. At home, Mama had always bought fabric from the peddler who came to our village.

"New in town?" the woman asked.

"Yes, ma'am," I answered in English, when Mama blushed and Libke looked down. I was proud to know the right words.

The girl looked up from her spools.

Mama pointed to two dark, plain bolts of woolen fabric, and the woman laid them on the counter for her to touch. "We'll get this sturdy gray for Anshel's shirt," Mama decided quickly, fingering a coarse fabric. "You girls can choose your own. But pick something woolen for winter, and agree on just one." She smiled at our excited faces. "I can piece the fabric out and use less if your dresses are of the same cloth."

After living in my dull gray, scratchy dress for so many weeks, I wanted a light color. My eyes kept going back to a soft tan scattered over with red flowers. Libke liked a plaid, gray and black with patches of yellow. We murmured intensely to each other in Yiddish.

"The tan will show every smudge!" Libke objected. "And it's almost winter."

"But I'm so tired of dark colors," I groaned. "Especially gray! What's your second favorite?"

Finally, we settled on a deep blue covered with green vines and leaves. It was my second favorite and Libke's third favorite, but she gave in. I loved it so much! It was soft to the touch and beautiful, like a forest at dusk. Neither of us had ever had a dress made of anything so fine.

The girl plunked her elbows on the counter next to the bolt of cloth, fingered it, and looked at us.

"That won't wear well," she said in English. "It's not a fabric for homestead girls."

"We wear it for school only," I answered. "We wear old dress at home."

She shrugged. "Don't say I didn't warn you. Don't come back and complain that it snagged on the fence when you were feeding the hogs or something."

"Irene," said the lady. "Can you tidy the ribbons for me, please?"

The girl went back to her work. Feeding the hogs! I thought, smiling to myself. Ha! Not my family.

Mama, Papa, and Anshel were at the front with a stack of supplies. The twins stood on tiptoes, gazing at bright jars of candy on the front counter.

"We picked our cloth, Mama!" I called happily in Yiddish. She fingered it and nodded her approval.

"Tell the lady we need eight yards, Shoshana. And matching thread."

"Eight," I told the lady, holding up eight fingers in case I remembered the word wrong. "And . . ." I didn't know the word for thread, so I just pointed.

The thin woman smiled. "Thread, yes. It's very pretty fabric, isn't it? I grew up on a farm myself!" she said.

"Mother!" objected Irene. "You don't have to announce that to everyone."

Mrs. Huber laughed. "There's no shame in it, Irene! You did too, until five years ago. Don't you remember how much you and Clive liked to paddle in the horse pond when you were small?"

Irene blushed. "Oh, that was such a long time ago, Mother! I'm a town girl now."

"A ribbon to match?" Mrs. Huber asked, holding one up. "This blue would look pretty in your hair, and your sister's."

Mama hadn't said anything about new ribbons. "No, ma'am," I said shyly.

Just then, a broad-shouldered man with suspenders over a red plaid shirt came from the back of the store. A burly boy about Anshel's age, with a sullen face, slouched behind him.

"You here, Rozumny?" the man said to Papa. "Surprised to see you back with money in your pockets."

"Good morning, Mr. Huber," Papa said politely. "Let me introduce my family. They have come all the way across the sea to join me. My wife, Mirele, and my daughters, Libke and Shoshana, my big girls, and the little ones, Pearlie and Tsivia."

Mr. Huber hitched his trousers up. "Five more mouths to feed, eh? Just in time for winter."

"Yes. We're getting prepared for winter and next spring," said Papa. "Could you ring this up? Also the fabric. And six sticks of candy, one each for the children and my wife."

He switched back into Yiddish. "Have you decided what kind you want, *mamele?*" He lifted Tsivia in his arms, and she pointed to a pale pink stick with red stripes, then hid her face against his shoulder.

"I want lellow!" Pearlie shouted, pointing. The boy reached two sticks of candy out of the jar.

"Hold up, Clive," called Mr. Huber. Pearlie jumped, trying to reach the candy, but the boy held it out of her reach. "You have cash, Rozumny?"

"Cash?" Papa looked confused. "Some. Enough to cover most of it. Put the rest on account, please."

"Sorry. No can do," said Mr. Huber. His lips twisted slightly into a grin.

"*Vos iz dos*—What's going on?" Papa demanded, going red, his Yiddish accent getting stronger. "All the farmers round here have accounts."

"Can't do it, Rozumny. New policy. I don't keep accounts for Yids. Can't give you credit. Can't trust you'll pay me back."

"I been shopping here for three years," Papa said angrily. "Always paid up. And you treat me like this now? When I have my whole family here?"

Mr. Huber's cheeks were flushed, making the pale stubble on them stand out more sharply. "That's your own lookout. Got me own family to feed. Can't be feeding yourn at my expense."

"You still want the candy?" asked the boy.

"Yes," said Papa. My little sisters took their candy and sucked silently, looking worried. I could pretty much understand everything Mr. Huber had said. I didn't think Mama could, but she knew Papa was upset.

Papa turned to Mama and murmured to her in Yiddish. He started figuring rapidly on a scrap of paper.

"Put this back for now, Anshel," he said, pointing at the sack of flour. "Get another sack of cornmeal instead. That's cheaper. Put back the sugar. And the work gloves. And this." He pointed to a pail. He hesitated over a pane of glass. "No, we'll keep this. I want to replace our window. Glass will keep the cold out better."

"I don't need candy, Papa," I said.

"Me neither," murmured Libke.

"I don't want any," said Anshel.

Papa looked embarrassed. "I'll get candy for all of you another day, soon. I promise."

Mama looked at the two of us sadly. "Libke, Shoshana," she said. "I'm very sorry, but I have to put back your cloth. I'll still make you new dresses. But if I make them and Anshel's shirt out of the same fabric, I can manage with less. And his fabric is cheaper." She started back to the fabric counter.

"We'll just take this then," Papa said curtly.

"Yah," said Mr. Huber. He punched numbers into a machine. "Load 'em up, Clive."

The boy lifted a sack and headed out for Papa's wagon.

"I have a bit of cash left over after all," Papa said, trying to smile. "Shoshana? Libotshka?" He stroked my sister's head. "Anshel? Some American candy? Peppermint? Or butterscotch?"

I didn't know what those were. But all three of us shook our heads. Right then, I felt as if candy from that store would choke me.

Eleven

After the general store, Papa had to stop at the blacksmith's. By the time we got home, it was nearly dusk. Both our little sisters were asleep, their faces sticky. Anshel sat silently against the other side of the wagon, his long legs stretched out in the straw, a dark silhouette against the dusk. I picked up Pearlie, and Libke took Tsivia, and we carried them into the dugout to bed. I peered out the door to see if things needed to be carried in. Papa and Anshel had taken the feed and tools into the barn and seen to the animals. Anshel heaved the last sack of cornmeal from the wagon and lugged it into the house.

Mama started the fire. Libke adjusted the blanket over Pearlie, who was fussing. I fed Zissel, dipped water for her out of the bucket, and watched her settle down on the pallet at the twins' feet. Papa lit the lamp.

"That's odd," Papa said behind me. "Mirele, did you decide to get the second fabric for the girls after all?"

Mama got up from her knees in front of the fire and dusted her skirt. "No," she said. "I only got the gray. That's all they charged us for."

We all looked at the table. The sunbonnets and the coarse gray fabric Mama had chosen for Anshel were there, up out of the dirt, and so was the blue-and-green woolen fabric that Libke and I had chosen. I reached out to touch it. It was as soft and lovely as before, so much nicer than the rough cloth for Anshel's work shirt. The flickering lamplight brought out subtle colors in the deep blue, a shimmer of silver, a flicker of gold, a shimmer of pale pink.

"Maybe Mr. Huber changed his mind and let you have credit after all, Papa!" I said. "Maybe Mrs. Huber said he should. Did he give you the sack of flour too?"

"No," Anshel said. "Just the cornmeal."

"It's a mistake," said Papa flatly. "The bill wouldn't have come out right with the fabric added in. The boy must have loaded it into our wagon by mistake."

"Are you sure, Papa?" I'd been imagining going to school in a dress made of that beautiful cloth, feeling it against my wrists and neck, soft and comforting and luxurious, watching the sunlight bring out its colors.

Papa dug in his pocket and handed me the paper with the price calculations. He was right. The total only came out to what he had paid with the dress fabric subtracted. And even if Mr. Huber had somehow changed his mind about the credit, he certainly wouldn't give anything away for free. Even I was sure of that.

"Now I'll have to miss a half day's work tomorrow driving to town and back just to return it," Papa said. "When I was planning to fix the plow."

I hadn't said a word about not getting candy. I'd said no when Papa offered it to us again. I'd watched Tsivia suck on her pink stick and Pearlie lick the yellow one dreamily without asking for a single taste, even when they swapped licks with each other. I hadn't said a word when Mama said we couldn't buy the cloth we had chosen, and that I would have to wear another gray dress. If Papa didn't have enough money, he just didn't. I knew clothes and candy weren't the most important things to buy, especially with winter coming. But now the cloth was there in our home, on our table, glimmering in the light of our fire, just as if it were meant for us. For me and Libke. So we could look pretty at school.

I knew I shouldn't say anything now either. I knew it, but I just couldn't help it. "It's not *fair*, Papa," I burst out. "You shouldn't have to take it back. It was the Hubers' mistake. Other people wouldn't spend half a workday taking it back. I just know they wouldn't. Can't we just keep the fabric since they put it in our wagon? Please?"

Papa's dark eyebrows drew together and his voice seemed to deepen. "No, Shoshana. You know better than that. It isn't ours to keep."

"And you know what they'd say if we did that," Anshel said. "Just like back in Ukraine."

"They'd say, 'Those cheating Jews.'" Papa said darkly. "We have to be even more honest than other people. If we aren't, they blame our whole race."

I took a last look at the cloth on the table. Someone would have a dress made out of it one day. But it wouldn't be me.

Twelve

We helped Mama make up Anshel's new shirt and our two dresses. I wasn't as good with a needle as Mama and Libke, so I did the easy parts, cutting out and basting and hemming. The cloth was crisp and new and plenty sturdy, sturdy enough to do chores in even, although Libke and I planned to save ours just for school to keep them nice. I tried to be happy that I would soon have a brand-new dress. I was, I really was, but I couldn't help remembering the soft blue-green woolen fabric that Papa had taken back to Mr. Huber.

"Huber stared and turned red, and then he shouted at his son," Papa told us at supper, after he got back. "But he didn't thank me."

"The wife didn't either?" Mama asked. "She seemed like a pleasant woman."

"She wasn't in the shop when I went by," Papa said.

"Mrs. Huber *was* nice," I said. "She told me she grew up on a farm."

"The Hubers have land not far off, as well as the store," Papa said. "Two full sections, all paid up. His wife's brother runs it with some farmhands. Huber sends his son out to help at planting and harvest time."

"That girl, Irene, she doesn't like farming," I said. "Irene said the fabric was too good for homesteaders. She wasn't so nice. She thought we kept pigs!" I burst out giggling, and everyone else smiled too.

"Pigs?" asked Pearlie.

"A big animal with a short nose, and short legs," I said. "And a curly tail. Christians keep them because they eat them, but we don't."

Pearlie nodded her head, chewing. "I not eating pig," she said with her mouth full. "This is bread!"

When Mama had finished the last buttonholes, she said we could go to school the next day.

Libke was restless that night. "Will you sit with me and help me if I don't remember an English word?" she whispered, when we were in bed.

"Of course. If I know it. Sometimes when I don't, I just change the sentence around and say things a different way. Anyway, Hirsh said you were a very good student. Remember?"

"Yes, but not like you."

It wasn't usual for me to be better at anything than Libke, but it was true. Learning English came to me more easily. It wasn't really fair, either, because Libke studied harder. "Do you think the girls will be friendly?" I asked. "That girl Irene in the store—she didn't like us, I don't think."

"Well, with a father like that!" Libke said.

"Her mother was friendly, though. Couldn't she be like her mother?"

"She's only one girl, anyway," said Libke.

Tsivia murmured in her sleep and turned over, making the hay rustle. Outside, something howled. It was a wolf. I knew that now. But Papa had said they wouldn't bother us here, not with a strong door, not with Berchik guarding us. Eventually, I fell into an uneasy sleep.

Libke and I held hands on our way to school the next morning. We took turns carrying our lunch pail, because after a while it dug into our palms. Anshel walked us the first mile and then showed us how to follow a ridge the rest of the way. Squinting against the broad blue sky, I saw the clustered bright colors of girls' dresses against a large sod building. The white shirts and pinafores of running children flashed in the sunlight. The teacher came out onto the front step and rang a bell. We hurried down the ridge as the other children lined up. Two boys in overalls came running across the prairie from the other side of the schoolhouse, so we weren't the very last in line.

"You're new, girls? And maybe not from this country?" The teacher spoke slowly and clearly, and she smiled at us as the others took their seats at wooden desks. She was small and delicate, with vivid dark eyes and neatly coiled light-brown hair. "I am Miss Jansen. Evie, you go sit with Grace. You two girls sit here." She patted a desk and we sat down. "I'll come talk with you in a bit."

Inside, the sod schoolhouse was clean and freshly whitewashed, with a scrubbed wooden floor. A glass window on each side let in plenty of light. I saw Irene Huber, the storekeeper's daughter, in the third row of desks. She kept her head facing forward and didn't glance at us even once, though I knew she must have heard Miss Jansen talking to us when we came in. The kids stood and sang a song Libke and I had never heard. Then they got out books and slates and set to work. Three little ones came forward and read out letters as the teacher pointed. She explained things in a gentle voice when they made mistakes. I was pretty sure I was going to like her.

Miss Jansen drilled another group of children on geography, pointing at a globe. When they sat back down, she summoned me and Libke to her desk.

"Hello, girls," she said, slowly and clearly. "What are your names?"

"My name is Shoshana. Her name Libke," I answered promptly.

Miss Jansen smiled. "Hello, Shoshana. Let's let Libke say her own name. What is your name?" she asked Libke.

"My name ees Libke," said Libke timidly.

"Hello, Libke and Shoshana. And how old are you?"

"I am eleven," I said. "My *shvester* is . . ." I clapped my hand over my mouth.

"I am vorteen," said Libke.

Miss Jansen asked us more questions and had us read out of an easy book. Reading English was much harder than talking. The letters were different from Yiddish letters, and they went backwards, left to right, the opposite of the way Yiddish and Hebrew went.

"Good," said Miss Jansen after a while. "I'm sure you'll soon be speaking English just like all the other children. Don't worry if it's hard at first. Many come here speaking other languages. I'll start you together in the third McGuffey reader."

She walked over to a shelf and handed us two worn, tan-colored books. She opened one to page fifteen. "See if you can understand some of this story, 'Johnny's First Snowstorm.' You know what 'snow' is?"

Libke nodded vigorously. "*Yo*. We know 'snow.' Hirsh, our teacher, he tell us this word *snow*. Where we come from, is much snow."

"Is much snow in Nordakota?" I asked, proud that I could ask her in English.

"North Dakota," Miss Jansen said with emphasis. "Say it after me."

"North Dakota," I repeated, blushing a little. So I had that wrong.

"Yes. We have lots of snow in North Dakota," Miss Jansen said. "Try reading the story."

We went back to our desk and struggled together. From time to time, the girl named Evie peeked at us over her shoulder and grinned. I liked the way freckles spread over her cheeks and across her snub pink nose. I smiled back, then dropped my eyes and looked down at my book.

"Lunch," announced Miss Jansen after a while, and the kids all scrambled to the cloakroom in the back and out the door.

I stood with Libke on the schoolhouse steps. A group of boys were digging into lunch pails in the scant shadow of the schoolhouse. Little kids dropped theirs by the school and ran around shouting. A small girl's lunch pail tipped over and she ran back to it, righted it, and peeked at me from under uneven bangs. Then she ran off again. Two groups of older girls sat by the little stream that trickled past the schoolhouse. One tall girl bent over the stream and reached into it, pulling out a bottle. She shook her fingers. "Ooh! Cold!"

I looked at Libke.

"Should we sit with them?" I whispered.

"I don't know," Libke whispered back.

I was so glad I wasn't alone. I was so glad I had my sister.

We walked a little closer. Nobody looked our way, so I found us a spot by the stream near a clump of willow shrub. We sat down, spreading our skirts on the grass.

"Hey!" The freckled girl who'd been peeking at us during lessons came running over. "Come sit with us!" She had a broad smile and a cute gap between her two front teeth. "I'm Evie."

"I'm Shoshana," I said, getting up. "This is my *shvester*, Libke."

"Move over. Make room," Evie called to her group. "How old are you, Shoshana? Twelve, like me?"

"Eleven," I said. "Libke vorteen."

The other girls made room for us in their circle. We unwrapped our lunches. A grasshopper leapt over my foot, startling me.

"These are Grace, Milly, and Irene," Evie said, pointing around the circle. Grace and Milly smiled. Irene looked down at the soft white bread and cheese on a cloth napkin in her lap.

"We meet Irene in store," I said.

"Oh, yes," said Evie. "Everyone goes to Huber's sooner or later. I love going in for supplies. Irene gets a ride here in a buggy, did you know? Usually her brother Clive takes her. She's kind of a princess, this town girl!" She grinned, nudging Irene, who lifted her chin.

"I can't be walking out here all this way, now that we live in town! My Pa says next year or maybe the one after, they'll be building a school in Shakton," Irene announced. "A real fine one. Then you can have this country school all to yourselves."

"Oh, Irene!" Milly moaned. "We'll miss you! Won't you miss us?"

"Anyhow, you're on the claim next to ours, you know, Shosh, Shosh . . . how do you say your name?" Evie asked.

"Shoshana," I said.

"Shoshana and Libby. They're on the old McIvor claim, you know?" she asked the other girls. "Anshel's sisters, right?

We know Anshel from school last year. Milly wanted him to stay on for another year or two, didn't you, Milly?" She grinned.

Milly's face turned pink. "Well, it seemed like he wanted to graduate," she protested. "And he was good at his lessons."

I watched and listened, understanding bits here and there, feeling startled. Milly knew Anshel and knew he had wanted to stay in school? And she thought he was handsome, it seemed, from the color of her cheeks. I'd never considered my brother that way before.

"I've been wanting to visit you," Evie went on. "Mama always has so many chores for me, though, and she says when the weather gets colder is time enough to go visiting. I'm so glad there's a new girl nearby my age. Frances, my big sister," she gestured with her chin at the group of older girls, "she won't hardly talk to me anymore, not when there's anyone better around, she says. She and her friends are so snooty. Where are you from, anyway?" Evie stopped long enough to take a breath. "You know, you can do what we do and put your bottles here in the stream, between those rocks there, to keep them cool. I hate lukewarm milk! I don't like milk all that much in the first place. But I'm a champion milker anyhow! The fastest in my family. I can beat Papa and Frances both, and even Mama, hands down!"

"That is clever idea, bottle in stream. Tomorrow we do," I said, trying to understand her rapid words. "We come from Liubashevka. In Ukraine. The Russian Empire. Long, long way."

"It sure is! We learned Russia in geography. It's huge! You know, you talk pretty good. Does she?" Evie gestured at Libke.

"Yes, Libke can talk English. Some."

"I talk, yes," Libke said. "Just, Evie talk very fast."

Grace and Milly laughed, and so did Evie. "She hardly lets any of us get a word in edgewise, sometimes," Grace said. "You'll get used to her. What's in your lunch? Is that fish?"

"Fish!" exclaimed Milly. "Around here?"

"We have a little left we bring from home," I said. "It is—I don't know the word. Put in salt and sour . . ."

"Pickled? Pickled fish! I never heard of that before," said Evie. "Is it good?"

"Yes, very good. You want taste?"

I held out my bread and herring.

Irene put a handkerchief to her nose and turned her head away. "It smells disgusting," she said. "Your breath is going to stink if you eat that, Evie. Just like the new girls'."

Did my breath stink? I put up my hand and checked. I didn't think so.

"Ignore her, Shoshana," Libke murmured in Yiddish. I guess she could tell what Irene had said, or at least she had noticed Irene's expression and her handkerchief and knew what they meant. Milly, who was sitting next to Libke, giggled at the sounds of the Yiddish, and imitated them in a noisy whisper to Irene.

Evie scowled at Milly and took a tiny bite of fish. "Um . . . interesting," she said, after she swallowed it. She took a swig of milk. "Do you want a bite of gingerbread?"

"Oh, I do!" said Milly. "I love your Mama's gingerbread."

Evie took out a large chunk of cake and broke it into smaller pieces, handing one to each of the girls except Milly.

"Oh, come on, Evie! I didn't mean any harm! Pretty, pretty please?" begged Milly, with her hand outstretched, and after a pause, Evie gave her the last chunk.

I bit into mine. It was soft and moist, and a surprising prickle stung my nose. And it was sweet, so sweet! Libke nudged me and shook her head. What was the matter? Why wasn't she eating hers? I smiled at Evie and took another big bite.

"So who else is in your family?" Evie asked. "You and Libby and Anshel and your Mama and Papa?"

Something flew over Evie's head into the stream, and water sprayed over us. Irene scooted back, shaking droplets off her dress. "Watch where you're kicking that, Lars!" she shouted.

Two small boys jumped into the stream with their overall legs rolled up and splashed toward the ball, laughing.

"Sorry!" called Lars, heaving himself up onto the bank and running off.

"No," I said. "Our family has more. Two baby sister. Tsivia and Pearlie."

"Oh, you're so lucky!" said Milly. "I wish I had a little sister! And you have two!"

"That's what you think," said Grace. "It's a lot of extra work, minding little sisters."

"Poor Gracie has three little sisters," Evie said. "They drive her crazy. So, five kids in your family?"

Irene shuddered. "I simply couldn't bear that," she said. "It must get so crowded and dirty in a homesteading shack. That's what you live in, right?"

"Not shack. A dugout," I said proudly. "Papa and Anshel build it. And not only us in the dugout. Also Zissel and Berchik."

"*Seven* kids in your dugout?" Evie exclaimed. "I only have Frances. Are those two brothers or sisters?"

I laughed. "No, Berchik is dog. Zissel is my kitten."

Grace and Milly and Irene stared at us. Evie jumped to her feet just as Miss Jansen came out on the steps and rang the school bell. "No! You can't! How can you have one? You have a kitten, Shoshana? I can't believe it. It's not fair! I'm coming over with my Mama this very Sunday afternoon! You have three sisters, nice ones who talk to you—not like my sister—plus a brother and a dog *and* a kitten? Where on earth did you get a kitten? Did you bring it all the way from Looba—what did you call it?—from Ukraine?"

Thirteen

"You shouldn't have eaten the cake Evie gave us," Libke scolded on the way home.

"Why not? It was rude, you not eating yours. We always used to share with our friends at home."

"But these girls aren't Jews. You don't know what fat that cake was made with."

I hadn't thought about that when I took the cake. "It was butter," I said hesitantly.

"How do you know?"

"I could taste it. Sweet cake wouldn't be any good with schmaltz. It would smell like chicken! Nobody would make it that way."

"Are you sure it was butter? Then maybe I could eat mine." Libke looked longingly at the lunch pail, where she had tucked her piece of gingerbread. "But I heard that Christians some-times cook with pig fat."

"Pig fat? That sounds like a rumor," I said staunchly. But was she right? I felt a little sick. Had I eaten food we weren't supposed to eat?

"Libke, it didn't taste like meat at all!" I insisted. "It was butter. Evie told me they have four cows. They must have more butter than they know what to do with!"

We passed Papa and Anshel working in a field, not far off. Papa took off his hat and waved it. Berchik came bounding toward us, leaping over the tall grasses like a dolphin leaping through the sea.

"Still . . ." Libke said. "You can't be quite sure. What if they greased the pan with pig fat?" She reached into the pail, sniffed the gingerbread, then hurled it toward Berchik, who gobbled it.

"Libke! You could have given it to me!" I complained. "I'm hungry!"

I ran ahead into the dugout. "We have a new friend at school, Mama!" I cried. "They live on the next claim. She said she'll come calling with her mother on Sunday afternoon. I'll help you put together the samovar!"

Libke came in behind me and dropped her reader on the table.

I seized Zissel, who was curled on top of Mama and Papa's bed where the twins were napping, and kissed her all over. "My friend wants to meet you, little *ketsele!*"

"*Nu!*" Mama seemed startled. "Our first American visitors! What's the girl's name?"

"Evie Pedersen. Can we bake honey cake on Sunday morning?"

"Not unless those hens of ours start laying more eggs, *nudnik*! We're lucky if we get enough each week to make challah."

Mama ruffled my hair. "We'll make something else nice. How was school for you, Libke?"

Libke dipped herself a ladle full of water. "The teacher is kind. We ate lunch with Evie and her friends."

"What about the lessons?" asked Mama. "Were they hard?"

"Arithmetic was easy," Libke said. "And English—I think we'll learn."

"Of course we will," I said excitedly. "Why shouldn't we? Does Papa have any sugar cubes we can serve Evie and her mother with their tea, Mama?"

By Sunday afternoon, our floor was swept as clean as we could make it, the cast-iron stove was well scoured, and Mama and Papa's bed was made up tightly. I had polished the new glass window with a rag until it gleamed. Papa and Anshel were out in the fields. The rest of us had on clean, fresh clothes with just-brushed hair. Libke and I wore our new school dresses. My old pink hair ribbon was pretty raggedy-looking by now, because I had used it to play with Zissel, even though Libke had warned me not to, and we couldn't find Pearlie's ribbon at all. Libke's beautifully embroidered blue hair ribbon and Tsivia's were as crisp as ever after Libke pressed them. They both wore them in their silken hair. Mama had on her best dark wool dress, and her hair was neatly tied up under her headscarf.

"Mama," I said. "Now that we're in America, maybe you should wear a hat instead of a *shtern-tikhl*."

Mama smoothed a fresh, flower-embroidered cloth over the rough wooden table. "I don't need anything fancy right now," she said. "When we have money for fancy, I'll buy you girls that fabric you wanted."

"*And* a hat for you?" I asked. I wanted a pretty dress from the forest-at-dusk fabric, but I wanted Mama to look like an American too.

"Maybe. Go ahead and get the samovar out of the trunk, will you, girls?"

Libke and I unwrapped the shiny samovar pieces from layers of quilts, and Mama carefully put it back together. I fetched water from the well to fill it. Mama put fuel into the center and started the water heating.

The brass samovar looked glorious on the tablecloth. I had complained, shlepping the huge trunk, about all the things we were bringing, but now the samovar made me happy. Seeing it shining on the table was almost like being home again. We had no sugar cubes for the tea, but Mama took a surprise out of the trunk—a jar of last summer's homemade raspberry jam!

"I know the trunk was heavy," Mama said a bit apologetically, "But after all our work picking *di malines* and making jam in the hot weather, I just couldn't bear to leave it behind."

"I didn't see you put the jam in, Mama!" I was delighted. We could have that with our tea and the challah that was left from yesterday.

I remembered picking those raspberries by the edge of the forest last summer, reaching through prickles, carefully avoiding the bees, the sun beating hot on our heads and surrounding us with the scent of fruit. I couldn't wait to taste it again, to taste home. But it was more important to be sure there was plenty for our visitors.

"Don't eat too much jam, Pearlie and Tsivia," I warned my little sisters. "We need most of it for Evie and her Mama. They are our *khosheve gest*! Our very first guests in America!"

"And we want to have some left in case any of us gets a fever this winter," Mama added. "Tea with raspberry jam is the best thing for fever."

Pearlie had been running in and out all morning, keeping watch. She ran out with Berchik again, then burst back in. "A horse is coming!" she shouted.

We all hurried outside. A buggy drawn by a bay horse was coming from a long way off, disappearing for a few minutes as the tracks dipped down below the level, then reappearing again as they came back up.

Evie and a woman in a neat tea-colored print dress climbed out, each of them carrying a large basket.

"Velcome!" Mama said, smiling.

Mrs. Pedersen set down her basket and gave Mama a kiss. She had a broad face and freckled pink cheeks, with a smile like Evie's.

"I should have come before," she said heartily. "The hamper is food for your family. Evie's basket too." We all looked down. The basket was packed with bright glass jars filled with what looked like canned vegetables and fruits.

"Oh!" Mama clasped her hands over her heart. "So kind! So much thank!"

Suddenly I remembered our mezuzah. Would Evie see that and think my family was different and strange?

"Good afternoon, Mrs. Rozumny," Evie said politely. "Hello, Libby. Hello, Shoshana." She looked around excitedly. "Where's the kitten? Inside?"

"Yes," I said, drawing her toward the dugout. As we went through the door, I stood on the right, blocking the mezuzah from view. "I keep Zissel inside. So she not be gone when you visit."

Evie set her basket down on our table. It was also full of good things to eat, including a loaf of soft white bread and eggs carefully nestled in a towel. Zissel leapt off the bed and slipped underneath as everyone came in, hiding from the unfamiliar voices. Evie squatted by the bed. "Come here, kitty! Nice kitty! What's her name again?"

"Zissel. She likely come out soon."

But Evie didn't want to wait. She flopped at full length on the floor and reached under the bed, her stockinged legs sticking out. "Come out, Zissel!"

"Be careful!" I warned. "Sharp claws!"

Evie crept under the bed a little way. "I don't care!" said her muffled voice.

Mrs. Pedersen turned around. "Evie!" she exclaimed. "That's no way to behave while visiting. Get up right now and act like a lady!"

Evie reluctantly wiggled back out again and stood up, tugging her dress down. It was a pretty brown-and-pink print, and it didn't show the dirt much. I helped her brush herself off.

Libke finished setting the table, and we all sat down. Mama put tea in the teapot, turned the spigot to fill it with hot water from the samovar, and set it on the top.

"Oh, my!" said Mrs. Pedersen admiringly. "I've never seen such a contraption before. That's how you make tea in your country?"

"*Yo.*" Mama nodded, a bit tongue-tied. "Make . . . make vera gut tea."

Mama poured us each a glass, adding lots of hot water to mine so it would be the way I liked it. She showed Mrs. Pedersen and Evie how to stir jam into the tea.

"Hey!" Evie whispered to me, after stirring in a big spoonful of raspberry jam and taking a sip. "I thought it would taste weird. But it's delicious!"

"And braided egg bread!" Mrs. Pedersen said, accepting a slice. "I haven't had this in a very long time."

"We call it *challah*," said Libke.

Mrs. Pedersen nibbled. "Very tasty."

"It's so light," Evie said. "Like cake, almost!"

Mrs. Pedersen and Mama were busy talking about chickens. When Mama, with some help from Libke, explained that it was a good week when Papa's hens laid four eggs, Mrs. Pedersen promised to come again soon and bring us chicks. "The chicks are already feathered in. You can raise a brood this fall," she said. "And by next spring, they'll be laying. Meanwhile, I brought you some provisions. To help you through your first winter."

"Oh!" Mama clapped her hand over her mouth when she understood. "Very kind! Very kind! And the food! Libke," Mama tugged my sister's arm, switching into Yiddish. "Please tell her *a groysn dank* from me and Shmuel for everything."

"Of course," Mrs. Pedersen smiled, when Libke translated Mama's thanks. "We all help each other. It's the Christian thing to do. Shmuel is Mr. Rozumny, your husband?" She looked around as if expecting to see him.

"Papa work in field," I said. "Our brother Anshel too."

"Working?" Mrs. Pedersen looked shocked. "On the Sabbath?"

"Oh! Sunday not our Sabbath," I explained, relieved. I had thought Mrs. Pedersen was offended that Papa wasn't there to meet her. "Saturday our Shabbos. We're Jewish."

"Jewish," said Mrs. Pedersen slowly. "And you're still going to be Jewish here in America?" she asked Mama. "You could try our church. It's full of good people!"

Mama looked bewildered. Something soft bumped my ankle from behind. I looked down. Zissel's little black-and-white face looked up at me. I nudged Evie and pointed.

"Mama, may we be excused?" I asked in Yiddish. "We want to go outside and play with Zissel."

Mama looked nervous about trying to talk without us, but she nodded. "Girls and cat play," she explained to Mrs. Pedersen, before switching back into Yiddish. "Remember, girls, you are wearing your best dresses! Keep them clean!"

"Yes, Evie told me you have a kitten! Such good fortune around here, where cats are so scarce! I hope she'll grow up to be a good mouser."

"She will, I know!" Evie said. "Look at her big ears. That's a sign of a good mouser, my auntie Laura says."

"Zissel too little catch mice," I said. "But soon she catch!"

Mama and Mrs. Pedersen sipped their tea while the rest of us burst outside into the sunshine. Berchik came racing toward us, barking his happy bark. Zissel scrambled onto my shoulder. I giggled.

"Is she afraid of the dog?" Evie called. "I wish she would climb on me!"

"Not afraid. Just because he bark," I said.

Berchik raced toward us, then away and back again. Pearlie tossed a clump of grass. Berchik seized it and shook it fiercely in his jaws.

"Berchik fight the grass!" I told Evie.

Evie reached over to stroke Zissel. "Can I have a turn to hold her?"

I plucked Zissel down from my shoulder and cradled her in my hands, crooning to her in English for the first time. "This is Evie, Zissel. She want hold you."

"Hi, Zissel," Evie said softly.

Libke came close on the other side. "She like touch head very soft," Libke said.

Evie tried it with one finger. "Oh, she's purring!" Her face lit up with happiness. "I wish I lived here with you!" She sat down carefully on the grass. The twins immediately plopped down on either side of her. Libke and I sat too. Berchik flopped beside us, panting.

Evie carefully set Zissel in her lap, and broke off a long stalk of grass. She waved it in Zissel's face. Zissel batted at it. Pearlie and Tsivia giggled, and Pearlie grabbed for another stalk.

"*Kum aher*, Zissel!" she called. Zissel leapt after Pearlie's stalk and then veered off to pounce on a grasshopper.

Evie waved her grass stem in a circle, and Zissel ran after it, round and round, until she tumbled over. We laughed.

Zissel licked her paws, recovering her dignity.

"What do you think of school?" asked Evie. "Do you like Miss Jansen? I love her little butterfly brooch. You didn't see her wear it yet. She didn't wear it this week. Do you have any brooches? Or rings? I have one my auntie gave me. I wear it to church."

Evie was back to talking a mile a minute now that we were outside and not having to behave like ladies. I only understood the beginning.

"I like Miss Jansen," I said.

"Yes, Miss Jansen is kind," Libke said. "She go slow. She say word two, three time."

"She's patient, yes. Your English is already getting better in just one week! Hey, stop! The dog!"

Berchik poked his nose over Tsivia's leg and sniffed at Zissel. Zissel started, leapt off Tsivia's lap into the grass outside the circle, and disappeared. The tall grass stems rippled above her as she ran off.

"Catch her! What if she gets lost?" Evie jumped up.

Tsivia patted Evie's pink-and-brown skirt soothingly.

"No worry," Libke said.

"She go off many time," I said. "She come back."

Mama came to the open door of the dugout. "Girls!" she called in Yiddish. "Come say goodbye to Mrs. Pedersen. It's time for them to go."

We headed back in, leaving the door open to the outside sunshine. Mrs. Pedersen smiled at us all, brushing a bit of grass out of Evie's hair.

"Thank you for the tea, Mrs. Rozumny," said Evie. "It was all delicious."

"And so nice to see how lovely you have made your home here," added Mrs. Pedersen. "So clean and snug. Do let me know if you change your mind about visiting our church. And meeting some good Christian people."

"I wish we could live in a dugout," said Evie. "It's so cozy. Why can't we, Mama?"

Mrs. Pedersen smiled. "I lived in one with my family when I was a little girl," she said. "It does have advantages. Cool in summer and warm in winter."

"We never live dugout before," Mama said. "In Liubashevka, in Ukraine, we have wood house."

"Hey!" Evie pointed at the doorway. "Your cat came back!" I squinted into the sun. There was Zissel, a dark shape against the brightness.

She trotted forward, carrying something in her mouth, her head and tail held high. It was a new, triumphant way of walking, with a strut in her step that I hadn't seen before.

She paused at Mrs. Pedersen's feet and dropped something. Mrs. Pedersen jumped back. Tsivia shrieked. We all looked.

A dead mouse.

"Oh!" exclaimed Mrs. Pedersen.

Fourteen

The second time Papa gave me a fiddle lesson, Berchik howled by the door again, asking to be let out. I didn't like the mocking way Anshel laughed when Berchik did that. So I took to practicing in the barn. Papa came out sometimes to help, and the oxen and Royt were good company, snorting quietly, shuffling in their stalls, and munching hay.

I could hear that the fiddle didn't sound the same way when I played it that it did when Papa played. When the bow was in my hand, it just didn't make the music that made me feel as if I were back home in Ukraine. It didn't bring me the feeling of the women chattering while they scrubbed clothing under the drooping willows on the riverbank, white buckwheat blooming in the farm fields, a bowl of ripe cherries on the table, the scent filling our dark cottage. When I played, I only saw what was in front of me. I only felt the fingers of my left hand awkwardly grasping the neck of the fiddle while with my right hand I drew down the bow, trying with all my might to do it smoothly and with the right tension and the right speed. But I kept trying. I practiced nearly every day. After a few weeks, I was getting better at staying in tune. I didn't need Papa's chalk marks for my fingers as much anymore. Drawing the bow so that the strings sang instead of screeching was the really hard part, but I wasn't screeching as much of the time as I had at first.

Papa was helping me learn "*Oyfn Pripetshik*," a song about children starting school. He had played it often for us back at home in Ukraine. I loved the warm reverberations of the sounds the fiddle made when I drew the bow down correctly, and I loved the peace in the barn. Often, Zissel came with me when I milked the cow, and she stayed afterwards. She wasn't like Berchik—she didn't seem to mind the sounds of me learning. When I had finished my after-school chores, I often stayed with the animals for an hour or so, playing the fiddle to the shuffling, munching oxen and watching the sun go down through the open barn door.

In school, sometimes all the scholars stood and sang songs together. I liked that, though I didn't know the words. One day, Miss Jansen handed me and Libke a songbook so we could follow along.

"Singing is a wonderful way to learn English," Miss Jansen explained. "It helps you remember. I have found that with many of my scholars. Nils here," she smiled at a boy about Libke's age with flyaway, stick-straight fair hair, "Nils could sing whole songs before he was willing to say any sentences at all!"

Singing was all right, but my voice wasn't sweet and true like Libke's, and I liked playing the fiddle better. I wished Papa would drop by the barn and give me another fiddle lesson, playing the song himself to teach me how it should sound, filling the barn with the feeling of Liubashevka, but he wouldn't be doing that anytime soon. He had gone to visit the Kantors to talk with them and some of the other Jewish men living nearby about new farming methods and about the business of the Jewish Agriculturalist Aid Society. So I was working by myself. Some days I sounded better and some days worse, but I kept on trying.

In the beginning of November, Miss Jansen caught me reading ahead of the page she had assigned to me and Libke. I had raced through the silly poem about a white kitten. There was a much more interesting story later in the book about an elephant.

"I'm very sorry, Miss Jansen," I apologized, my voice quavering. "I already read the kitten poem. Truly."

"Shoshana," Miss Jansen asked. "What does the kitten poem teach us?"

"Stay inside. Stay out dirt," I said. "But that foolish. Because how we farm and keep house clean and not get dirty?"

Miss Jansen's lips twitched. "And how did the boy weigh the elephant, in the other story?"

"He put elephant in boat. Saw where water go. How high on boat. Then same with rocks."

"That's right," she said. "Very good. I believe you are ready for the fourth reader."

"Libke also?" I asked. "Libke is older."

"Libke is doing fine work in the third reader," said Miss Jansen. "Everyone learns at her own pace. Libke, you stick with that book for now."

"Yes, Miss Jansen," Libke said.

I glanced at her apologetically, after Miss Jansen left.

"I don't mind, Shoshana," she whispered in Yiddish. "Not as long as we can still sit together." She bent her head over the third reader again.

Libke worked so hard at her reading. I had a tendency to look out the window and daydream about the stories without realizing I was doing it until Miss Jansen came up beside me and tapped on my book. But Libke was the head of the class in arithmetic, even better than the oldest girls, Evie's big sister Frances and her friends, who were nearly ready to graduate and who hardly talked to anyone who wasn't in their lunch circle.

Libke was better in arithmetic than the oldest boys too, when they came back to school for winter term. That wasn't hard, though.

Before, the oldest boy in the class had been Nils. He was a thin, friendly boy with a limp. He had broken his left ankle in the summer and it was still healing, he had told Libke one day at lunch when we were fishing our milk bottles out of the stream. He wouldn't be much help with the farmwork until his ankle was stronger. At recess, he usually sat huddled against the schoolhouse wall, the sun whitening his startlingly fair hair, and read. I'd noticed that sometimes he looked over at our group, though, and especially at Libke. I'd wondered if he was lonely. But even if he was, the new boys at school clearly weren't his friends. They were bigger—and meaner.

These new boys, Mac and Fred and Clive Huber, Irene's brother, were about fifteen or sixteen. They were back at school now that the harvest was over. Mac and Fred helped their fathers farm. Clive worked with his uncle Edward, who was farming the Huber land. At recess, sometimes the three of them kicked the ball the little boys were playing with far away, or stole it altogether and guffawed. Once, one of them snatched Nils's cap off while he was reading and threw it on top of the schoolhouse. Nils just shrugged, limped his way up the bank and onto the roof, and got it down. Mostly the big boys left Nils and the rest of us alone. But they were loud and rude during lessons, and they didn't listen to Miss Jansen.

The only good thing about having the older boys at school was that Clive hitched his horse, Domino, to a post by the schoolyard. Clive and his friends often went off somewhere at noontime. Whenever they were away, I spent time with Domino. Domino was beautiful, a glossy black with a diamond of white on his nose. It wasn't long before he would come to me when I called and let me pet his white spot. I didn't dare do it when Clive was around, though.

Domino was much too nice a horse for that Clive. I wanted to ride him across the prairie with the wind in my hair. I imagined myself grooming him in our stable. Domino would have been so much happier belonging to me, I was sure.

The three older boys were strong from farmwork. All three of them were as tall as men. They whistled, scuffled in the back of the classroom, flicked ink at each other, and tipped over desks. Clive Huber's specialty was swallowing air and making loud burping noises.

I felt uneasy now in school. I tried not to look at them. I kept my eyes intent on my lessons when they made rude noises or knocked things over. I pretended not to notice when they kicked the smaller boys' balls off into the tall grasses. Once, little Lars shouted at them, and Mac shoved his face into the dirt. When Lars got up, his eyes were furious and his lip was bleeding.

"Bully!" Lars shouted. He reminded me of a fierce, cornered cat fighting back against a much bigger creature.

Mac laughed as if Lars had given him a compliment.

My heart thudded so hard I felt my pulse pounding in my fingertips. But I kept my eyes down. I didn't want those boys to turn on me. Later, when Fred and Mac and Clive had gone off, I wet my handkerchief in the cold stream and gave it to Lars to hold on his swollen lip. But I still felt hot and ashamed that I hadn't tried to stop Mac when he was hurting little Lars.

"Those big boys make lots trouble," I whispered to the other girls, when I sat back down. Then I remembered that Clive was Irene's brother. But Irene just shrugged.

Milly laughed. "They're just being funny, trying to make school more interesting. And Clive," she lowered her voice to a whisper. "He's kind of good-looking, don't you think? With that floppy hair over his eyes?"

"Clive?" I asked incredulously. "No! His horse good-looking, yes! More than good-looking. Beautiful!"

"That Domino of his," Irene said dismissively. "Clive likes animals more than people, Mama says. I guess that's why he likes working on the farm so much. We'd hardly ever see Clive if he didn't come into town mornings to deliver milk and eggs to the hotel and then drive me out to school. Whenever he has an excuse, though, he goes to the farm instead of school. I tell him he's going to grow up plain ignorant! He just shrugs and says he knows all he needs to know."

A week or so later, the three smallest children, Lars and Emily and Betsy, were at the front of the class, sounding out words with Miss Jansen.

"D, U, C, K," said Miss Jansen patiently, naming the letters. "Take the letters one at a time, Betsy. What sound does D make?"

"Duh," whispered Betsy. "Duh, uh . . ."

A loud burp came from the back of the room. A long, mocking, jeering kind of burp.

Giggles broke out.

Miss Jansen frowned. "Quiet, in the back!" she said firmly. "You are interrupting the lesson!"

"I'm very sorry, Miss Jansen," Clive said meekly, but grinning. "I suffer from dyspepsia."

"Endeavor to control yourself," said Miss Jansen. "Remember what 'C, K' says, Betsy?"

"Quack, quack!" whispered Lars helpfully.

"D, U, M!" said Clive loudly. "Dumb! Like Betsy!" Mac and Fred chortled.

Betsy started to cry. "I don't know it," she wailed.

Miss Jansen patted Betsy's shoulder. "Ignore those silly boys," she murmured.

My pulse pounded in my temples. Suddenly, I couldn't take it one more minute. I turned around and glared at Clive.

"Ha! You think 'D, U, M' spells dumb? And you oldest in the school! Who is not smart now?" Miss Jansen had explained to me and Libke just last week that the word "dumb" ended with a silent letter "B." And we had only just started learning English!

"Shut up," muttered Clive. "Oh, it's you, Jew girl, you and your sister? Fellas, those are the Yids. The ones who came into my Pa's store. And expected credit!"

"Quiet, class!" snapped Miss Jansen.

I shrank back into my seat. What had I done? Now I knew trouble was coming.

The next morning, Libke hurried ahead of me on the path. The pale early morning sun lit up the crisp, embroidered blue ribbon she wore in her hair every day and the blue plaid shawl wrapped closely around her. Libke somehow always managed to look neat and pretty.

"Hurry!" she urged me. "I don't want to be tardy!"

Was that the only reason she was in a hurry? Some mornings when we were waiting outside the schoolhouse, I had caught her peeking at Nils, and he often seemed to be watching her. But it was getting harder and harder for the two of us to be early to school. We had to hurry through chores and breakfast now that the sun was rising later. And the mornings were frosty.

I slipped on a slick patch of ice and nearly fell. I caught up with Libke, my boots crunching through the frozen grass. "Miss Jansen should really do something about those big boys," I said. "I can't stand them. Why do they get away with everything?"

"They're awful," Libke answered, out of breath. "But what can Miss Jansen do if they won't pay attention? She's not that much older than us."

"She should punish them," I said firmly. "To keep order."

Zissel jumped out of a shrub beside the path and raced through the frozen tufts of dried grass alongside us. She had started doing that lately. Sometimes she was even there to meet us on the way home from school.

"Isn't Zissel cute?" I asked. "She's not a baby anymore. She's almost a big girl cat! Look, she wants to go to school with us!"

"How can Miss Jansen punish them, Shoshi? Make them stand in the corner the way she made that girl Mamie when she sassed her? What if they refused?"

"She could thrash them," I said hesitantly. There was a long stick in the corner of the cloakroom, left over from the previous teacher.

"You don't want Miss Jansen to hit anyone! That would be terrible! Anyhow, those three boys are all so much bigger than she is. They might fight back."

I plucked a branch off a shrub and waved it, watching Zissel jump. "They're such hoodlums," I muttered. "Why do they even bother coming to school?"

"Their parents make them, I guess. Hurry! Any minute, Miss Jansen will ring the bell!"

I stroked my cat one last time. "Go home, Zissel!" I called. "See you this afternoon!"

We ran to the end of the girls' line in the schoolyard, our panting breath making clouds in the air. When we were inside, I was glad to see a fire glowing in the schoolroom stove.

It was later that morning, when Miss Jansen had the middle girls up at the front, working with the globe, that I first noticed something was wrong with Libke.

"And what continent is this, girls?" Miss Jansen asked, setting her finger on Antarctica.

I raised my hand and looked at Libke. I knew she knew that too. We had studied together. But her hand wasn't raised. She was clutching her belly, and she looked pale.

"Excuse me, Miss Jansen," Libke said breathlessly, and she hurried out to the privy.

When Libke hurried out a second time, I watched her, feeling worried. As she passed the back row, she fell, sprawling onto the floor. A big, booted foot pulled in quickly.

"Let me help you up, Miss," said Mac, with mock gallantry.

For a moment, his back blocked my view. When Libke hurried out the door, her hair had come loose and was falling around her face. The boys were snickering and passing something. Clive slid his hand into his pocket, grinning. He had a black eye that morning, I noticed, a bad one. The purple stain spread halfway down his cheek. His face looked even more unpleasant than usual, splotched like that.

Libke got past them safely as she came back in.

"Are you all right?" I whispered, as she sat down. "Do you need to go home?"

Libke shook her head.

"Excuse me, Miss Jansen," Clive said in a high, mincing voice. He clutched at his belly the way Libke had done. "I need to run to the privy. For the second time this morning!"

Libke ducked her head, her cheeks burning.

"Ignore him!" I whispered fiercely. "He's an ignoramus!"

A few minutes later, Clive burst back into the schoolroom.

"Excuse me again, teacher!" he said in the high voice. Everyone turned to look at him. He held out a stick. Something dark and dripping dangled from it. "I fished this out of the privy. Libby's ribbon. I thought the Yids would want it back!"

He flicked his stick, tossing the ribbon onto our desk. Drops of privy filth sprayed onto Libke and me. With a chorus of "ews!" the girls around us ducked and shrank back. Libke's face went scarlet. She slid as far back on the bench as she could go.

Heat flared in me. I jumped to my feet, snatched the stick out of Clive's hand, and flung first the ribbon and then the stick into the schoolroom stove. It hissed and twisted, catching fire.

"Libke not want now!" I shouted. "Miss Jansen, Libke ribbon did not fall out. Clive Huber pull it out. When Mac trip Libke and make her fall. Then Clive throw ribbon in privy!"

"Me? I fished it out of the sludge for them!" Clive whined. "Why's she blaming me?"

"Is that true, Clive? Mac?"

"Me? What would I do with a hair ribbon?" Clive pretended to primp himself in front of a mirror, and the boys laughed.

Miss Jansen tapped her fingers. "Did anyone else see Clive or Mac take Libke's ribbon?"

Nobody spoke. Lars shook his head and glanced apologetically at us.

"Then we must not cast blame. Go back to your work, scholars."

I sat down, feeling shaky and furious. Why did boys get away with everything?

At the end of the next lesson, Libke nudged me. "I have to go home," she mouthed.

I walked up to Miss Jansen's desk. "Libke isn't feeling well," I murmured. "I need walk home with her."

"Yes, of course," said Miss Jansen. She walked out with us into the cold. "I hope you feel better, Libke," she said gently. "I'm sorry about your ribbon."

"Libke sew flowers on that ribbon her own self!" I said indignantly. "She bring it all the way from home, from Liubashevka. Where she sew flowers with friends Rivka and Bela! Now she does not have any ribbon, all because of mean Clive!"

"I'm truly sorry, Libke," Miss Jansen said again.

"Dank you, Miss Jansen," said Libke miserably, ducking her head and crossing her wrists tightly against her belly.

"What's the matter?" I asked, as we trudged toward home. "I hate that Clive!"

"Don't worry about the ribbon, Shoshi. But my stomach hurts." Libke moaned softly. "I need to go *again*. Can you wait a minute?"

"Sure. There are some shrubs over there."

After a few minutes, Libke emerged from behind the shrubs, looking pale.

"Shoshi," she whispered. "I think I might be really sick."

"We're nearly home," I comforted her. "Mama knows how to help an upset stomach."

"But Shoshana, it isn't an upset stomach," Libke whispered. "Just now I saw. There's blood."

Fifteen

"Blood?" I stared at Libke, horrified, and bolted toward the house. "Mama, Mama!" I cried. "Come quickly. Libke's bleeding!"

Inside the dugout, the tang of freshly chopped onions made my eyes smart.

"An accident?" Mama gasped, pushed aside the pan of beans she was sifting, and ran to the door.

Pearlie looked up from the buttons she and Tsivia were arranging on top of Mama and Papa's bed.

"Libke bleeding?" Pearlie asked, screwing up her little face as if she were about to cry.

Tsivia let out a startled wail. "Libke hurt?"

Libke hurried in behind me, her face scarlet. "Hush, Shoshana! It's all right, Tsivia! Hush, Pearlie. Mama," she whispered, burying her head on Mama's shoulder. "Not an accident. I'm bleeding . . . down there." She let out a sob.

"Oh, that's all!" Mama's face cleared, and she pulled Libke into an embrace. Then she held her at arm's length, smiled, and tapped her cheek lightly with two fingers. "Mazel tov! This happens to all girls!"

"Why are you doing that to her face?" I demanded, bewildered.

"It's our tradition. My mother slapped me, but I won't do that to my girls. It's supposed to bring good fortune, blessings." Mama wiped her eyes with her apron. "I'm happy and proud, Libke," Mama said. "This is how girls' bodies grow and get ready to have babies, when the time comes. This is exactly what's supposed to happen as you grow."

"Only to girls?" I asked indignantly.

"Only girls."

"But why did it have to happen now, Mama?" Libke wailed. "Why at school?"

Mama shrugged. "It happens wherever you are, when your body decides it is time."

"But not to me, not if I don't want to," I said, startled. "Right?"

"It will happen to you too, one day, Shoshi," Mama said gently. "As girls grow older, they start to bleed once a month."

"Every month, forever and ever?" I demanded.

"Not forever. But until you're older than I am."

Libke rubbed her eyes. "Don't worry, Shoshi. I just didn't know why it ached. Mama says it's supposed to happen. I guess it's like when baby teeth come out."

"But it hurts, you said! Libke didn't feel well at school, Mama."

"*Ach*, I'm sorry," Mama said. "Sometimes a girl feels a little sore. Come, I'll show you how to keep yourself clean. Shoshana, take Perle and Tsivia out to play so that Libke can have privacy."

I sat outside with the twins. Clouds scudded across the sky. I clutched my shawl around me, watching my sisters running about in the tossing grass. Zissel pounced and they chased her, shrieking. Zissel was much too fast to catch, but sometimes she doubled back or stopped and rolled onto her back, waiting for my sisters to catch up.

I felt all mixed up inside and upset for Libke. Mama said this happened to all girls, every single month! I could tell from Libke's face that it was more than a little soreness.

But Mama also said it was how girls' bodies got ready to be mothers. I loved babies. I remembered holding the bundle that was tiny Josef, our next-door neighbor Malke's firstborn. His hair smelled so good, and his little pink cheek was so soft against my lips. His tiny hand closed around my finger, as if he especially liked me. And when he got bigger and laughed, everyone who heard it laughed with him. His joy was like sunshine in Malke's dark little cottage, like springtime.

I did want a baby of my own someday. But that was a long, long way off, even for my older sister. So why did Libke have to ache and bleed now?

It was so confusing. Boys didn't have to go through this. That was so unfair, I thought, suddenly furious. It was one of so many things that were easier for boys than girls.

But there wasn't anything I could do about it. I sat huddled in my shawl on the cold ground, with my arms around my knees, watching my joyful little sisters racing through the grass, and remembering the tender way Malke's face looked, holding baby Josef, as if he were the most precious thing that had ever existed in the whole history of the world.

Sixteen

When the sun reached the horizon, Mama still hadn't summoned us back in.

I called my sisters over. "Time to feed the chickens!" I said.

I took my sisters with me to the chicken coop and we fed and watered the chickens. The ones Mrs. Pedersen had given us were growing nicely, but only Papa's first two hens were laying. I shooed all of them away, the way Papa had taught me, and then I gathered the eggs. Egg, really. There was only one.

It was warm and peaceful in the barn. Royt had wandered back to her stall, and she was waiting to be milked. The late-afternoon light fell on her dappled red-and-white flank and danced on the floating hay motes.

"Catch it!" said Pearlie, and she and Tsivia darted around the barn, trying to grasp the sparkling dust.

Royt mooed when I came in, then took another mouthful of hay. Berchik was flopped on his side on a pile of hay in the corner. He got up, stretched slowly, and ambled over to greet my sisters.

Royt mooed at me again, more impatiently this time, and shuffled and stamped. I knew what she wanted, but I was still in my school dress.

"Can't you wait just a little while longer, Roytele?" I asked.

"MOOOOO!"

Royt was getting angry, and I couldn't blame her. Maybe I could manage in my good dress if I was careful. I tucked up my skirts and slung on an old apron that hung on a peg in the barn. I got down the milking stool. Royt switched her tail, stinging my face.

"Easy! Good girl, Roytele," I crooned. "Easy now." I washed her and started up the milking rhythm, and soon her milk came down, hissing into the pail.

Something soft nudged my left ankle. I looked over my shoulder.

"Hello, Zissel!" I said. "You want some?" I pointed one of Royt's teats in her direction and squeezed. Milk arced through the air in a thin stream, like spider silk. Zissel leapt toward it and lapped eagerly.

"I try that!" called Pearlie, running forward and crouching next to Zissel. "Pearlie is a cat! Meow!"

"No, stay back. Your dress will get wet. I'll give you some when I bring it in."

I peeked out of the barn. The dugout door was still closed. I set down the pail of milk, now nearly half full, and rinsed my hands again with the bucket and dipper we kept by the barn door.

"Do you want to hear me play the fiddle?" I asked. Tsivia and Pearlie wouldn't laugh if I screeched.

"Me play too?" Pearlie asked hopefully.

"Not yet," I said. "When you're bigger. Papa says *my* hands are only just barely big enough." I held my palm against her small one to show her the difference.

The day before, after practicing, I'd left the fiddle on a shelf in the barn. I shouldn't have, I realized, when I tried to tune it. The weather was cold enough now that the fiddle was quickly slipping out of tune. From now on, I'd have to bring it in at night after practicing and just ignore any jokes Anshel might make.

I played a bit of "*Oyfn Pripetshik*" for them, and that day it came out sweet and yearning, smooth, silky, like our river back home when the water was high and it was running fast, slipping over the stones. They clapped their little hands.

A sound came from outside. Berchik heaved himself to his feet, walked to the barn door, and looked out, his ears pricking up.

"I hear music in the sky!" Tsivia said. "Singing!"

We followed Berchik to the door. Zissel bounded out too. The enormous sky flamed crimson and pink, laced with swaths of gold. Deep mounds of charcoal-gray clouds loomed like mountains. High overhead, long dark ribbons of birds came from the north, beating and beating their mighty wings, battling the fierce wind. Their call rolled through the air, a low, crooning cry. "Krrrrrrr—ooo—ooee! Krrrrrrr—ooo—ooee!"

As they got closer overhead, their cries sounded less musical, and became wilder, more plaintive. When some flew lower, we could make out great gray bodies, powerful fingered wings, and long outstretched necks. Cranes! I had seen one or two in Ukraine, but never like this, never such tremendous numbers and such awe-inspiring flight. From time to time, I caught a glimpse of red streaking the top of a head. As one group passed over, another line appeared high in the northern sky, and then another and another, each made up of hundreds of birds, lines shaped like V's, or loopy like soft W's. The dark lines twisted and drifted, changing shape as we watched, like ribbons in water, looping, arcing, wavering, reforming. The sky was so deep, so vast here, it was dizzying. I felt as if I could fall into it.

And Tsivia was right. The sky was full of song. A ragged, rough-throated song, but it was song—wild and free. The cries of the cranes felt almost as if they were coming from within me.

As the last crane passed over, the cries faded, and then we could hear only the wind.

Pearlie put her arms out like the cranes and ran. "Look, Shoshi! I'm flying!"

Tsivia put her arms out too, beating them. "Krrrr—ooo—ooee!" she called, sounding remarkably like the cranes.

I stretched my arms out like my sisters, and I ran with them, feeling powerful, feeling free. Feeling almost as if I could fly.

"Krrr—oo—oeee!" I called back to Tsivia and Pearlie, laughing. The wind whipped my call up and away, twisting it up into the sky.

I loved the birds in their long lines far overhead. I loved the fire flaming in the clouds fading down into night.

I loved the edge of cold in the fall air, the way it filled me, down to my toes, with a tingling, wistful energy. I loved the worn shawl flowing out behind me, making me feel as if I too might lift up and fly away.

But I didn't want to fly away. I didn't want to go back to Liubashevka anymore. I thought about my beautiful silver white birches, I thought about my cat Ganef, cozy in Malke's lap or snuggled beside her baby boy, and I knew Ganef was all right, even though we had needed to leave her behind.

My heart swelled in my chest, loving Ganef, though she was so far away.

I loved our new animals here. I loved them fiercely. Our Zissel's indomitable little scowling cat face. The way Berchik thumped his tail on the ground when I petted him.

I loved my baby sisters, running in circles around me. I loved Papa and even Anshel, coming in from working in the fields, the tired oxen plodding ahead of them, eager for their warm barn and sweet hay. I loved the dugout, with Libke and Mama inside.

With a love that had a little sorrow in it, I loved that I didn't have my monthlies yet, the way Libke did, and that I could still run like this, like a little girl.

I loved the endless space around us, the wide openness of the prairie. I loved the vast, flat land, growing cooler as winter came on.

And I loved the wind. Murmuring, crooning, moaning, wailing. If North Dakota was one thing, it was wind. The wind that made me feel so alive, so free.

Mama opened the door. Golden light spilled out into the dusk.

"It's cold!" she called. "Come in!" Tsivia ran to Mama, followed by Zissel.

"I'll just get the milk and the egg we found, Mama," I called. "And the fiddle."

Pearlie tugged on my shawl. "I love flying like birds in the sky!"

I smiled at her. "Me too!" I said.

Pearlie gave a little skip. "I love Nordakota!" she said.

She looked up at me happily, waiting for my answer.

"Me too!" I wanted to say again, but then Libke came to the dugout door, silhouetted against the light, helping Tsivia take off her shoes, and everything that had happened to us at school came flooding back. What Clive Huber had done. Libke's ribbon drenched in the stinking filth of the privy. And the way he had said those words—"Jew girls!"—as if the words themselves were more distasteful than the soiled ribbon.

Pearlie's sweet little face, looking up at mine, was so joyful, so hopeful. I squeezed her hand and smiled, feeling my heart open up again to the beauty of my family, of our little dugout with its mezuzah, of the great, wild space around us.

"I love the prairie too," I said.

North Dakota wasn't just the beautiful, free prairie. But the prairie was what North Dakota meant to my little sister.

Pearlie ran along beside me. Berchik came trotting back to the barn with us.

"Shoshi?" said Pearlie. "Berchik like your music now. Berchik stay and listen."

I stood still, startled, looking at Berchik.

"You're right!" I said. "He didn't leave the barn when I started playing! I must be sounding better!"

Seventeen

Libke's monthlies were over after only a day and a half, she whispered to me the next night.

"That was easy!" Mama said when Libke told her. "But have some more tea with raspberry jam."

That was Mama's remedy for everything. And it did taste delicious. I wished she would give me some too, but she didn't. She was very careful with that jam.

"*A dank*, Mama." Libke took the mug Mama offered her. "But it *wasn't* so easy. It hurt." She rubbed her belly.

"*Ach*, I'm sorry. But you'll be ready now. Next time it will probably last longer. Eat up—good food makes you strong! When you're strong, a little hurting doesn't matter so much." Mama scooped sunny-yellow *kulesha* into Libke's bowl.

At lunch the next day, the three big boys walked over to where Libke and I were sitting by the stream with the other girls. My stomach went tight. What now?

"Hey, Uglies!" Clive said. "Catch!" He tossed a crumpled-up piece of paper onto Grace's lap.

Grace snatched it and smoothed it out as Fred and Mac and Clive walked away snickering. It was a piece of wrapping labeled "Huber's General Store," with a crude pencil sketch of a girl's face. She had huge eyes and wide, pursed-up lips. Underneath was the letter "M."

Irene laughed and so did Grace and Evie. "They got you dead to rights, Milly!" Irene said. "Always waiting for a kiss!"

Milly went pink, smiled, and tossed her hair. "Just shows what *they* think about looking at me!"

"Is there anything on the back?" Grace asked eagerly, flipping it over.

There was another drawing, unlabeled. It showed a long, scowling face with narrow eyes and a hooked nose. Wild scribbles ran all over the head. Two long points curved up out of the scribbles. It almost didn't look human. I couldn't make any sense out of it at all.

Irene snickered and then so did someone else. I looked up and grinned too, uncertain about the joke.

"What is it?" I asked.

"It's you, dummy!" said Irene. "That's your curly hair. Nobody else here has curly hair."

"I don't look like that!" I said. "Looks like an animal! What are those?" I didn't know the words. I gestured to my head, putting up two fingers.

"Horns," Irene said, as if it were obvious. "Jewish horns."

"What?" I half-laughed, confused. "Only animal have horns."

"That's poppycock, Irene," said Evie calmly. "It's a myth."

132

"No, I heard it too!" said Milly. "You probably have real small horns that you never even noticed under all that hair. Let me see." She reached for my head.

"No!" I jerked away, and tore up the paper into tiny shreds. "That stupid! Poppycock, like Evie says!"

"Hey, I wanted to keep that!" Milly said.

"Don't get all hurt over it, Shoshana," Irene said. "Just be glad you don't have Clive for your brother. Though at least he doesn't call me 'Yid.' I mean, why would he? He calls me 'Ugly' and 'Dog Face' and things like that."

"He calls you 'Dog Face?'" Evie grinned.

"Oh shut up, Evie Pedersen! I don't need it from you too!"

"Dog face is nice face," I said.

"You didn't see me getting upset, Shoshana," said Milly soothingly, looking curiously at my hair. "When boys do stuff like that, it just shows they're thinking about you. That's what my Ma says."

Miss Jansen came out on the schoolhouse steps and rang the bell.

"Don't let on that it bothers you," Libke said, too loudly, in Yiddish, as we scrambled to our feet. All she seemed to have understood was that the picture was meant to be me. "They don't know the difference between a girl and a cow? They're just trying to get us to react. If we don't, they'll stop annoying us."

I flushed. Why did she have to speak Yiddish now, in front of everybody? No wonder people thought we were different. That we had horns.

Evie looped her arm through mine. "Whatever Libke is saying, she's probably right," Evie said. "Don't mind those boys, Shoshana. I think you're really pretty. I love your curly dark hair."

"It's really not a big deal when the boys draw dumb pictures, Shoshana," said Milly. "They did a lot last year. Especially of me." She smiled.

That was easy for her to say. Her picture had just made her look as if she were waiting to be kissed. Not as if she wasn't human.

But worse than the picture was what Irene and Milly had said. They believed that nonsense too? That—what was the English word?—that poppycock?

"Libke," I asked hesitantly, some weeks later, as we were in the garden searching for the last pumpkins. "At school . . . could you not talk Yiddish anymore? Everybody else speaks English."

Libke stared at me, a small, greenish pumpkin between her hands. "But that means I can't talk, Shoshi!" She set the pumpkin in the basket and wiped her hand across her forehead, leaving a streak of dirt.

"You can. You know some English!"

"Not enough. If we can't talk Yiddish, we won't be able to talk at school!" Libke looked as if she were about to cry. "Don't you want to be able to talk to me?"

"It's not that." I shuffled my feet. "Well, if you have to talk Yiddish, could you whisper so the others don't hear?"

"Fine, Shoshana," Libke said stiffly. "If that's the way you want it." She picked up the basket of pumpkins and marched into the house. A cold wind stung my eyes. Beyond Libke, the sun dipped toward the horizon.

My stomach felt queasy. I had hurt my sister's feelings. But if we spoke Yiddish, the other kids would be thinking about us being Jewish all the time. And they already thought about it often enough.

That evening, the wind howled around the dugout. During the night it grew colder and colder. I huddled close to Libke for warmth, curling myself away from Pearlie's little feet, which, even in stockings, were always icy in winter. Mama threw an extra quilt over us, and I half-woke, noticing the warmth creeping over me. I woke up warm and cozy, tangled up with my sleeping sisters. But the air was cold. I could see my breath. And our new glass window was covered with intricate patterns of frost, whirls like grass fronds or feathers. When I ran out to do the morning chores, the pale sun shone on frost on the ground. I had to break the ice in Cantor and Muley's trough and in Royt's so that they could drink.

"It's getting cold," said Mama. "I saw a few old bricks in the barn. Tonight I'll heat them in the stove after supper, and we can all tuck them at the ends of our beds to keep our toes warm. Time for the four of you girls to start sleeping with your heads all at the same end."

"And it is time for me to make you a proper bed, up off the ground," Papa said. "Mr. Pedersen has some lumber to trade. I don't want my girls sleeping on the floor in winter. Not you either, Anshel. You should start putting your pallet up on the bench against the wall."

"Mama, could I skip school today?" Libke asked, after Anshel and Papa went out. "I'll help you at home."

"You feel unwell?" Mama squeezed her shoulder sympathetically, and the two of them shared a private look that made me suspect it was Libke's monthly time again.

I'd never been all alone on the prairie, so far away from the dugout, the way I was that morning, walking to school, swinging the lighter-than-usual lunch pail back and forth against my skirt. The white-coated grasses stretched away in waves, for mile after mile, all around me. A hawk circled overhead, keening. From below, the sun lit up its red-brown tail. Watching it, I felt tiny, a speck in all that vast space. I missed my sister.

Had Libke stayed home because her monthlies were making her achy, I wondered, or was it so Clive and the other boys wouldn't make fun of her if she had to hurry to the privy?

Or was it because I'd asked her to whisper if she needed to speak Yiddish? Was it my fault?

The low sun shone through the grass. Each stem and blade of grass was outlined in frosty white crystals, every single one on the prairie, as far as the eye could see. I picked one and breathed on it, watching the crystals melt.

The school bell rang a warning through the frosty air. I tossed the blade of grass aside and ran down the ridge to line up in front of the door.

"Where's Libby? Is she all right?" Evie asked eagerly in the cloakroom.

"Not feel good," I said.

"Oh." Evie sounded disappointed. "That's too bad. I brought her a present. Look!"

Evie held out a freckled hand and showed me a creased, dark-blue satin ribbon. "It's not the same color as the one she used to wear every day. But almost. It's not a hair ribbon. It goes around your throat."

"Thank you, Evie!" I hugged her. "Libke be so happy!"

"It matched a dress that I've grown out of. It'll look good with Libby's eyes. Tell her I hope she feels better." Miss Jansen rapped her pointer on her wooden desk, and we hurried to our seats. It was strange, having our desk all to myself

During morning lessons, the sky darkened outside the glass windows. Grass stems and sticks sailed by, and even one flailing sparrow, whirled by on the icy winds. It was chilly at my desk without a seatmate. I inched as closely as I could to the steady heat glowing from the schoolroom's potbellied stove.

At noon, Miss Jansen told us that we could eat and play quietly inside if we wanted to, instead of going out. The big boys went out anyway. A few of the smallest children went out after eating, but they soon came running back in with pink noses and cheeks.

"Miss Jansen," asked Grace, as we sat on the floor near the stove. "Can we start decorating the schoolroom for Christmas?"

"Oh, yes, Miss Jansen!" said Irene. "Can we cut out snowflakes?"

"I don't see why not." Miss Jansen tapped a hard-boiled egg on her desk to crack the shell. "You girls can get out paper after you finish your lunches."

"I have something else to decorate with too this year, Miss Jansen!" said Milly triumphantly. "I brought these from home." She flipped open her reader. A pile of brightly colored cards slipped out onto the floor.

Evie helped her gather them up. "Your mother let you keep last year's Christmas cards?"

"Yes! And I have lots of relatives in Boston who send them! Can we make cutouts and put them around on the school walls, Miss Jansen?"

All the girls crowded around, and even Miss Jansen picked a card and ran her finger admiringly over ornate scrolls surrounding a sleigh driven by a full-bellied, red-coated man. "Lovely!" she said. "That will look festive for our Christmas recital!"

"I have some cards at home," said Irene loudly. "Fancy ones, fancier than these! I can bring them in too. Papa has relatives in Chicago who send them to us. Chicago Christmas cards are the best!"

I stood a little apart from the others, feeling awkwardly aware that all the rest of them were Christians. Should I join in decorating for their holiday or not? What if I did or said the wrong thing?

Evie squeezed through the group of girls toward me. "I have the best idea!" she whispered. "Will you come outside? I know it's freezing, but it'll be worth it, I promise."

I nodded thankfully. Evie grabbed the cloth she always wrapped her lunch in and shook the crumbs into the stove. We pulled on our shawls and caps and mittens and went outside. Wind gusted. I took a deep breath of the icy blast, feeling more at home in the fresh air.

"What we are going to do?" I asked.

"Collect milkweed seeds!" Evie said excitedly. "I know where there are some nearby. We can paste them onto the cards to be Santa's beard. The girls will be so surprised!" She skipped down the path and started pawing through the brush. A branch snapped back against her face. "Ow! Drat. There it is. That's milkweed. Can you hold that cloth open for me?" Evie pulled her red mittens off and started busily stripping seeds from the milkweed pods.

"I can't wait for Christmas!" she said over her shoulder. "This year, I'm hoping Santa will bring me butterscotch candy—that's my favorite—and a toy horse. A dear little brown soft one, with a mane. I saw one in the general store. Ow, ow, ow! My fingers are going to fall off!" She blew on her hands and yanked her mittens back on. "Can you get us more while my fingers thaw? Do you want a toy horse too? I saw a black one in the store! I know how much you love Clive's Domino!"

I handed her the cloth, making sure not to spill the mound of milkweed, and slid off my own blue mittens.

"Christmas isn't our holiday," I muttered.

"You don't celebrate Christmas at all? Not even a tiny little bit?"

I stripped the soft milkweed off and watched the feathery seeds settle into the pile. "No. We have different holidays."

"That's so sad! I mean, on Christmas we have especially good food too—a roast goose or chicken, and mashed potatoes with so much butter, and a Christmas cake! Let's go back now. That's surely enough." Evie held the cloth closed tightly around the milkweed and we hurried back toward the schoolhouse. The wind blasted into our faces.

"Poor Shoshana not to have Christmas!" Evie shouted over her shoulder. "I guess Jews can't get presents on Christmas because they're sinful and don't love Baby Jesus. But that's not your fault. I'll bring some of my butterscotch candy to school after Christmas and you can share it. That way you'll have a little Christmas too!"

Evie yanked the door open, fighting against a blast of wind, and went into the schoolhouse. My face burned.

It was impossible to be annoyed with friendly, talkative Evie, who planned to share her precious candy with me.

But if a nice person like Evie felt sure that Jews were sinful, what did that mean?

I was so confused. I couldn't bear to think about it any more. I wished I didn't have to go back into the schoolhouse with all the Christmas decorating going on. I just wanted to go home.

Eighteen

Evie burst out of the schoolhouse at the end of the day, shouting goodbye to Grace and Milly, who were heading off in the other direction. Irene helped Clive hitch Domino to the buggy.

"Do you want to walk together?" Evie said. "Since you're by yourself today? I'll go the long way so we can go together."

"Yes!" I took a deep breath of fresh prairie air. The sun had emerged from behind the dark clouds. It was much warmer now than when we had gone out to gather milkweed. I sucked one finger, where I had somehow gotten a blister. I hadn't actually made any Christmas decorations. Instead, I'd popped open the last closed pods and made piles of milkweed fluff for the other girls to paste on.

"Maybe Zissel meets us on the path home," I called to Evie.

"She does that?" Evie ran on ahead.

"Sometime. Zissel want to go to school with me, be smart cat!"

Evie laughed and twirled around with her arms stretched out. "I get so cooped up being inside all day."

"Me too!" I said, twirling with her. When we were dizzy, we collapsed onto the grass.

"Look at the sky," said Evie. "It almost feels like you're flying, when you lie back and look up like this. Hey!" A prairie dog popped out of the ground nearby, and Evie sprang up and darted toward it. It slipped back into a hole at the last minute, and she came panting back.

"They're always too fast for me!" she complained.

"What you would do if you catch it?" I asked. "Your family eat it?"

"Yuck! No! I just want to see them up close. They're so cute." She twirled around again.

"Wait, Evie!" I laughed suddenly. "Milkweed in your hair!"

"Oh, no! I'm getting so old! Pluck it out!" Evie pretended to be distressed. "That's what my Mama says when I'm combing her hair and I find a white one. One day, if I keep pulling the white ones out, she won't have any hair left!"

I held the milkweed up on my fingertips and let it drift off into the wind.

As we turned a bend in the path, suddenly, directly in front of us, a hawk plummeted from the sky. Something gave an unearthly shriek and we saw what the hawk had captured—a little prairie dog, rearing and twisting, striking with its tiny claws. I screamed.

The hawk hopped back, fluttered up a little way, and dove again, plunging its claws a second time into the prairie dog's plump little body.

"Go away!" Evie and I ran forward, shouting, but the hawk didn't budge. When we were a little way off, we stood still, staring. Close up, the hawk was beautiful and terrible, with bright, fierce eyes and brown markings on its white chest. More slowly now, the prairie dog writhed. The hawk remained still, wings outstretched and quivering, clenching its talons. The prairie dog's cries faded. The sound of insects swelled up from the grass.

"Oh, the poor little thing," said Evie.

Feeling as if I might be sick, I ran past.

"Wait, Shoshana!" Evie hurried to catch up with me. "Don't be so upset. That's life on the prairie. There's lots more prairie dogs. And everything needs to eat."

I knew that was how nature was. But maybe because Evie and I had just been talking about how cute prairie dogs were, right before the hawk dove, my heart still throbbed wildly, horrified by what I had seen.

Dark clouds blew across the sky. The prairie light dimmed, as if the sun were going down, but it wasn't, not yet. I pulled my shawl close around me.

"I have to turn off here," Evie said after a while. "See you tomorrow. I hope Libke likes the ribbon. It'll look better once it's ironed. Bye!" She ran off down the ridge and across the prairie, along the line of her father's barbed-wire fence, turning to wave again when she was halfway across.

I waved back, shuddered, remembering the hawk, and hurried the rest of the way home.

I rushed through my chores, then grabbed the fiddle case and headed back out to the barn. The shadows were already getting long. Royt was in her stall, munching hay. I blew on my fingers to warm them and started to practice a new tune that Papa had taught me the week before, a wedding tune. I was getting a lot better. My fingers felt much more nimble, and I hardly ever screeched now. But even when the music came out smoothly, the way it did that evening, something felt wrong. It was frustrating, because I couldn't figure it out. Something in the sound was missing. What was it?

When I had played the tune through twice and was in the middle of it for the third time, Papa came through the barn door with Cantor and Muley. I stopped to see if he wanted help, but he shook his head and gestured to me to go on playing. After he had finished, he rinsed his hands at the bucket and sat down on a hay bale to listen.

When I came to the end of the tune, Papa nodded. "It's coming along nicely," he said.

I handed him the fiddle. "Now you play for me, Papa."

Papa shouldered the fiddle and took the bow into his big, calloused hand. And the feeling of Ukraine filled the barn. The feeling of Liubashevka. As Papa played, in my mind I could see a flowering chestnut tree, its bloom past, shedding pink petals onto the dirt road in front of our home. I saw a bride and groom lifted shoulder-high in chairs, making little cries of excitement and alarm, a mother dabbing at tears, men thudding each other's shoulders. As the bow stilled, I saw the wedding guests at long last straggling home, singing or weary, quiet, their hearts full.

"That was beautiful, Papa," I said when the last notes faded.

Motes of dust floated in the air, passing through the slanted light. Muley sighed. Papa set the fiddle down and stretched his arms.

"Do you ever miss home, Papa?" I asked. "Do you ever miss . . . being with other people like us? Not being different all the time?"

"Ah," Papa said. He patted the hay bale next to him. I sat, curling my feet up under me.

"Yes, of course, sometimes," he said slowly. "Especially at first. You don't know what it was like for Anshel and me when we had just arrived. We felt so alone, with Mama and you four girls and home so terribly far away. Then it was just me and Anshel, camping in the wagon, us and the stony soil and the loneliness and the howls of coyotes and the wailing wind. You need to remember how hard it was for your brother when he gets irritable sometimes. He suffered, missing his Mama. Missing all of you."

"Me?" I didn't believe it.

"Yes!" Papa smiled. "I think he missed you especially. He talked about you sometimes. And Anshel wasn't able to go to school much, because we were struggling so hard to get the farm going. He missed being with kids his own age."

I shrugged. Maybe Anshel *had* missed other boys. Papa had to be wrong about him missing me, though. If he had, he would be nicer to me now.

Papa leaned back in the hay. "But home. Yes, I remember the good things. Our people. Our friends. Motke and Beinish. Davening in shul. The holidays. Playing music together."

Papa sat forward, rubbed the back of his neck, and sighed.

"But I remember why we left too, Shoshana. The harsh restrictions on where we could live, what work we could do, where we could go. The laws keeping Jews from going to school. The boys forced into the army. The Cossacks. The pogroms. The tsar. It's easy to think only about the good things when you're far away. It's easy to remember being with our friends, our neighbors, other Jews. But Liubashevka was the beautiful things and the terrible things, all rolled up together."

"I suppose. Yes, I know. I do remember. But here, I'm just so tired of it—people always looking at us like we're so different." I jumped up and reached for the fiddle again. I tried the tune Papa had been playing, and he listened thoughtfully, tapping his feet. Something was still wrong. At the end, I stopped with a groan.

"When I play," I said, "there's something missing. I don't know what. It's like, it's all floating on the surface of a river, flowing smoothly but not going deep. When you play, sometimes it's happy, the music dances, but sometimes there's also a sob in it, a cry . . ."

"Ah." Papa said. "You want to learn the *krekhts*. Come. I'll teach you."

He took the fiddle again and stood up. "At the very end of the note," Papa drew the bow down, "you throw your fourth finger out. That's the *krekhts*. That sound like a moan."

I tried. But when I did it, it just shifted the note.

"No, no, stop right when you throw your finger down. Abruptly. And speed up the bow a little."

I tried over and over, biting my lip in frustration. Suddenly I got it.

"Yes, yes!" cried Papa.

I tried the whole tune again.

Yes! For the first time, I heard more than notes in my own music. I heard home. Liubashevka. I heard the love, the joy. But also pain. All mixed together, inseparable.

I played faster, harder, my heart grieving, my heart rejoicing. There—now!—was the gladness, the exultation, the yearning. And more! More! Then agony came. But then, just when it felt impossible, when it seemed as if even the angels must weep—just then, up! Up again, aching heart!—came a golden shaft of joy at precisely the right moment, a joy made deeper by the pain.

It was all coming from this old fiddle. From my own two hands.

Across the barn, I saw Papa smile and his eyes brim with tears.

Nineteen

"We need three big pickles tonight, girls," Mama said one night, as Papa was assembling the new bed he had made with Mr. Pedersen's lumber for me and my sisters. Libke and I were helping Mama get supper.

"Your turn to get pickles," Libke said, shaking out the tablecloth.

"It can't be my turn," I moaned. "Didn't I do it last time?"

"You know you didn't!" Libke said indignantly. "I did, and my fingers froze! They're still numb, practically!"

"And the time before, I did it," said Anshel, who was helping Papa. "It's your turn."

"It's no fun getting pickles in winter," I grumbled.

Anshel laughed. "You call this winter? Softie! You're in for a shock! It gets *so* much colder. Winds like you never felt in your life."

I scowled at Anshel. We'd been through winters back home in Ukraine that were plenty cold. He was just trying to scare us,

I decided. And show how tough he was, having lived through winters on the prairie before we got there.

"It's so dark in there, Mama!" I complained. "I hate going by myself!"

"I want to come! I want to get the pickles!" Pearlie offered, snuggling against my side.

I patted her hair. "Can she, Mama?"

"Me too!" Tsivia demanded.

"Pearlie can go with you, but wrap her up warmly. It's too cold outside for you, Tsiviale, with your weak chest. They'll be back in just a moment."

I tucked a thick shawl around Pearlie and a muffler around her head, while Tsivia fussed and complained.

The sun was only a red glow on the horizon when we set out for the barn. I had a lantern in one hand and a pail in the other. Pearlie clung to my elbow. A thin coating of dry snow covered the ground, blown about by the wind. We had to walk carefully. The dirt path to the barn had patches of ice on it, nearly invisible now in the twilight. The door of the lean-to creaked when I drew it open.

"Can you hold the lantern up for me, Pearlie?" I asked when we got down the steps. "Use both hands. Hold it steady, and only touch the handle."

Even with the pale glow of the lantern, the root cellar was dusky, filled with eerie, moving shadows. There were hardly any pickles left in the murky liquid in the barrel. In the near-dark of the root cellar, I groped for them blindly with the pickle fork.

Nothing. I could hardly bear to keep on trying. I was *so* cold. Finally, I speared one. I drew it up slowly, trying to maneuver the long pickle fork carefully despite my slippery mittens. But I bumped the edge of the barrel, and it plopped off and glided down again into the depths of the water.

"No!" I shouted, banging on the barrel in frustration.

"Bad pickle?" Pearlie asked.

Irritated as I was, she made me laugh. "Yes! Bad pickle! It fell off!"

The root cellar seemed to be getting smaller, the tangled roots of the grass clutching at my hair. Were there even three pickles left in this barrel? If there were, this wasn't the way to get them.

"Hang on, Pearlie," I said. "Give me the lantern."

She held it up in her little hands, and I set it on the shelf. "Can you hold my shawl?" I asked, bundling it off and handing it to her. "And my mittens?"

I shoved my sleeves as far up as they would go, pulled myself up over the edge of the barrel, and, bracing myself against the shock of the cold, plunged my arms and the bucket I was carrying as far down as I could into the deep, cloudy brine. Gasping and shuddering, I scooped around blindly, reaching with one hand and pushing the lumps I encountered into the bucket. When I couldn't stand it a moment longer, I drew up the heavy, sloshing bucket.

"Got some!" I told Pearlie triumphantly. "Thanks for helping!"

I grabbed the lantern, and we raced out into the fading light. A blast of wind howled, taking all the feeling away from my wet arms.

"I need my shawl, Pearlie! But keep my mittens," I said, my teeth chattering so much I could hardly get the words out. I set the bucket and lantern on the frozen ground and clumsily wrapped the shawl around myself. We hurried toward the house, smelling smoke from the chimney.

When we were nearly at the dugout, a dark shape bolted across the path. Zissel. Then Berchik pounced on her, growling playfully, out of the dusk. Startled, Pearlie grabbed at me. I slipped and fell, whacking my elbow on the hard ground. I lost my grip on the heavy bucket, and the icy contents sloshed all over the path and onto me and Pearlie. The lantern guttered and went out, plunging us into darkness. Pearlie wailed.

Mama burst out the door, took one look at Pearlie, and gathered her up in her arms. "What is going *on* here, Shoshana?" she cried, pulling Pearlie into the house.

I scrabbled around the dark, searching the frozen ground with my already frozen hands, grabbing up one pickle and then another. If there had ever been a third in the bucket, I couldn't find it. Sopping wet, shuddering with cold, I ran into the house.

Mama had already stripped the wet clothes off Pearlie, who was wailing in front of the stove, looking tiny, wrapped up in a thick blue blanket. A big pot of water was heating on the stove.

"What happened?" Mama demanded. "You're dripping too! Get those wet things off."

"Zissel and Berchik startled us," I explained, shivering. "I fell and spilled the pickles. I landed on my elbow. It hurts!" I rubbed it.

"I'll go check on the animals," Anshel said, getting up. "And I'll bring in Zissel and Berchik. It's going to turn cold tonight."

"Told you it was bad outside!" I muttered.

"But where did all that water come from?" Mama asked. "Hush, Perle, the bath is almost ready! Libke, can you fetch the tin tub? Tsivia, stay back from the stove. Shoshana, get that dress off! You're soaking!"

"I know, Mama!" I said. I pulled off my wet things and wrapped myself in the blanket Libke held out. Didn't Mama even care about my elbow?

"There were hardly any left," I said in a small voice. "I couldn't get any with the fork. So I just rolled up my sleeves and scooped some up in a bucket."

"Oh, Shoshana, don't you ever think?" Mama groaned, kneeling down to chafe Pearlie's skin gently with a wet washcloth in the bath. "That's so unsanitary!"

Tsivia reached into the tub, grabbed one of Pearlie's hands and licked it, then dug in her small teeth. Pearlie screamed and hit her.

"Tsivia, no!" said Libke.

"Pearlie taste like pickle!" Tsivia said smugly. "I clean because I stay in the house!"

"Don't hit your sister, Perle," Mama groaned. "Don't you get wet too, Tsivia. Libke, can't you keep her away?"

153

"My arms aren't so filthy!" I said, feeling terrible. "And they were the very last pickles anyway."

"I think they probably were, Mama," said Libke.

"So they all spilled in the dirt?" asked Mama, helping Pearlie get out and into a warm towel.

"I picked them up," I said. "They're in the bucket."

"Well, Perle's finished in the bath. Wash yourself off, change into something dry, and I'll start a new pot for the soup. You can rinse off the pickles. Supper will be late tonight." Mama sighed. "Really, Shoshana," she started, in an irritated voice. She stopped, took a few deep breaths, and started again, more quietly. "Shoshana, you must learn to think ahead. Look at all the trouble this caused."

I felt as bad as if I'd done it on purpose.

Anshel came in, along with Berchik and Zissel, who were acting as if they hadn't been the cause of everything.

Pearlie ran toward Berchik in her nightgown. "Bad, bad, bad, bad dog!" she scolded in her high little voice. "Bump Shoshi, make Shoshi fall down!"

I picked her up and hugged her. At least Pearlie was on my side. "We can't tell him that now," I said. "Dogs don't remember things like that very long. By now, he doesn't even know what you're scolding him for."

Pearlie wriggled down and hugged Berchik. Libke and I put supper on the table.

"These pickles taste watery," Anshel said, after biting into a slice.

"Shoshana wash them!" Pearlie said.

"Wash pickles? Shoshana, I don't expect you to be a great cook or anything, but who washes pickles? Oh, right. You dropped them."

I glared at Anshel. I wished I never had to hear another word about pickles ever again in my entire life.

But the next morning, after bundling myself up as warmly as I could to go milk Royt, I ran into Anshel just outside the dugout door. He was examining the patch of ground where I had spilled the pickles. I could still smell the brine.

"What, Anshel?" I asked, irritated. "Did I miss a pickle in the dark? Sor-reee! Do we have to keep talking about it today too? I didn't mean to get Pearlie all wet! She wasn't any wetter than I was, and nobody cared about that, or my bruised elbow. Anyway, Pearlie's fine now!"

"Calm down! Nothing's wrong," Anshel said, grinning at me. "Don't be such a spitfire! Look, Shoshana. Where you spilled the pickles, there's no ice."

It was true. Although the path was icy everywhere else, there it was bare, just earth tinged slightly green.

"Huh!" I said, looking at it more closely. "From the salt and vinegar, I guess."

"No one will slip now coming out the front door," Anshel said, running his foot back and forth over the bare part. "It's a good thing you got impatient and scooped up that whole bucketful after all!"

"Hey! We could use the rest of the pickle brine when we want to melt ice sometime," I said.

"Right," said Anshel. "And we have a whole barrelful. We'd have to just dump it anyway, since you can't use it twice, right?"

"Why are you asking me? I thought you said I was a terrible cook!"

Anshel smiled and punched me gently, the way he used to when we were small, back in Ukraine. "I was only teasing, Shoshi."

I punched him back. Maybe he wasn't so bad after all. "Well, you're right, you can't use it twice. It isn't strong enough, after having pickles soaking in it."

"That brine'll be useful when the cold weather comes."

I didn't say anything about how cold it was already. Anshel and I both squatted down and touched the earth. Cold. Damp. Pickle-smelling. Greenish. But not frozen at all.

Twenty

Libke didn't go to school the next day either. That afternoon when I got home, Papa was hitching the oxen to the wagon.

"Hurry, Shoshana," he called. "You're coming to Shakton with me. I have to get a piece for the plow. Mama has an errand for you."

"I need thread to match that scrap of fabric on the table," Mama explained, poking at the fire and sitting back on her heels in front of the stove. Tsivia and Pearlie both immediately tried to sit on her lap, shoving at each other. Mama wobbled, nearly toppling over backwards. "No, girls!" she scolded wearily. "Mama is busy. Libke, can you distract them? I simply can't trust your Papa to get that right," she told me. "One time I did, and he brought me dark-blue thread instead of black!"

"I guess his eyes aren't as sharp as yours," I said, pocketing the piece of fabric.

"I want to go to Shakton!" Pearlie shouted.

"Me too! I want to go too!" said Tsivia.

157

"Only Shoshana is going today. Come," said Libke, settling on our new bed. "I'll tell you both a Malgrim the goat story. One day, Malgrim decided he was lonely and needed a friend . . ."

Tsivia ran over and climbed up next to Libke, but Pearlie yanked on my skirt. "I want to go with Shoshi! Please, Mama?"

Mama straightened up, dusting herself off and wiping her hand over her forehead. "Well . . . would you mind taking her with you, Shoshana? She's been fussy all day. It might help to get her out."

"I don't mind. Come on, Pearlie, where's your shawl? It's cold."

The sun was sinking fast as Papa urged the oxen along the rutted path. I tied Pearlie's shawl tightly around her, and then wrapped my shawl around me and Pearlie both. Her little body was warm against mine. She wriggled nonstop and kept up a constant chatter.

"Rabbit! Nother rabbit! See? I can run fast like rabbit. I can hop. Hop, hop! I will get lellow in Shakton? I can get lellow? Papa, Papa, I can get lellow?"

"Lellow? Do you understand what she means, Shoshana?" he asked.

I remembered suddenly. "Candy! Yellow candy! Pearlie, *meshugene*, silly one, we don't get candy every time we go to town!"

Papa laughed. "You know, Shoshana, I do owe you, Anshel, and Libke a stick of candy each. I promised. And to keep the little ones from fussing, you can buy them a stick to share. We'll save half for Tsivia. What do you say?"

"Yes, Papa!"

I hadn't had candy since I couldn't remember when. Sometime years ago in Liubashevka. And if I had to go into Huber's anyway to get the thread, I might as well get candy too, since Papa was offering!

Papa drove the wagon straight to the blacksmith's at the far end of Main Street, where it petered out into the prairie.

"Hurry," he said, handing me a coin. "Everything will be closing soon. I'll meet you outside Huber's when I'm done."

I didn't like this end of Main Street much. The blacksmith's was at the far end, past the sidewalk, with nothing on the other side and only the depot and empty lots between it and the saloon.

I took Pearlie's little hand in mine. A wind rushed down the road through the dusk, whisking grit into my eyes. As we approached the saloon, I heard loud music. A crude, hand-lettered sign in the window read No INDIANS.

What a horrible sign. I couldn't see why anyone would want to go in anyway, but it must feel like being spat on, seeing signs like that. I pulled Pearlie across the road.

The saloon door swung open, letting out a cloud of cigarette smoke and raucous laughter. A man stumbled out. "Whoa, Nellie!" he yahooed. "Watch yourself!" I couldn't tell if he was talking to himself or me. He hooted foolishly and nearly fell over his own feet.

"Come on, Pearlie," I murmured. We hurried onto the plank sidewalk and along to the general store.

"I hope it's Mrs. Huber, not Mr. Huber, tending the store," I whispered to my sister. "She's much nicer."

Pearlie nodded solemnly. But it wasn't either one of them.

Irene Huber stood behind the cash register, twisting her hair idly around her finger. She was watching a small boy and a girl about my age with long, dark braids. They had their backs to us and were examining a shelf of toys.

"I said, no touching!" Irene called sharply. "Do you even have any money? If you're not going to buy anything, you have to go."

The girl pulled her brother's hand away from a toy clown and whispered something to him.

Irene was certainly in a bad mood. Had the little boy just broken something? I took Pearlie's hand again so I could keep her from doing that.

"Hello, Irene," I said warily.

"Oh, hi, Shoshana. Is that your baby sister?"

"Say, 'Hello, Irene,' Pearlie." I whispered in Yiddish, emphasizing the English words.

But Pearlie didn't even try. "I want lellow! Shoshi, Shoshi, Papa said yes I get lellow!" she announced loudly in Yiddish.

"She doesn't talk English?" Irene sounded incredulous.

I blushed. "Not yet. She's saying she wants a lemon candy stick. But first, my Mama wants thread the same gray as this cloth. That's what we came for."

Irene found a spool of thread for Mama. I held it up to the light, compared carefully, and nodded.

"Are you getting candy too?" Irene asked, lifting the lid of the glass jar, reaching in with tongs, and setting Pearlie's lemon candy stick on a piece of paper. Looking at the candy seemed to be putting her in a better mood. "What flavor do you want?"

"I'm getting three. One each for Libke and Anshel and me. I never had it. What's the best kind?"

Irene leaned eagerly over the jar. "Well, I love the lavender and also the rose! Those are the pale purple ones and the pink ones. They're so refined! Evie likes butterscotch, those are the gold ones with the brown stripe. Milly likes all of them."

"Do you get to eat candy anytime you want?"

Irene sighed. "No. I wish! Pa says I'd eat up all the merchandise."

The candy sticks gleamed in the jar. I chose the dark-green wintergreen for Anshel and the reddish-purple clove flavor for Libke. For me, I picked butterscotch. The combination of gold and brown looked simply irresistible.

As Pearlie and I went out, the girl with long braids and her brother approached the counter. "Yes?" I heard Irene ask coldly. "We don't give credit to Indians, you know."

They were Dakota? So that was why she was being that way. I glanced over my shoulder, then realized it was rude to stare.

Pearlie sat next to me on the bench outside the store. I broke the yellow stick into two pieces, as evenly as I could, and gave one part to Pearlie.

She stuck the piece into her mouth and gave a deep sigh of contentment. I sniffed the other three sticks and then quickly licked each one. Had I picked the best one for myself? Yes, I decided happily. I liked butterscotch the best.

The Dakota girl and her brother came out of the shop door. The girl's face was set and she kept her eyes straight ahead, but her little brother peeked at Pearlie curiously.

Pearlie took the candy out of her mouth and beamed beatifically at him. "*Sholem aleykhem!*" she said.

I nudged her. "He doesn't understand Yiddish!"

"My sister says hello," I explained in English to the little boy, who was grinning back at Pearlie.

His sister looked over, unsmiling, her dark eyes wary. She was about Libke's age. Instead of a shawl, she held a vividly striped blanket around herself.

"Hi," I said. "I'm Shoshana. That's my sister, Pearlie. Oh!"

I'd only just noticed the small leather drawstring bag the girl held. I'd never seen anything like it. In the center, intricately worked in beads, was a figure I recognized. A large bird, with extended, fingered wings. A stretched-out blue-gray neck. A noble head, a patch of white, a flash of red above. The beads glimmered in the angled late-afternoon light. The image felt so alive, so real, I almost expected it to take flight.

"A crane!" I murmured.

Pearlie was looking too. "Krrr—oo—ooee!" she called, stretching out her arms, her candy clutched stickily in one hand. "Krrr—oo—ooee!"

A moment later, Pearlie and the little boy were running up and down the sidewalk, arms reaching out, calling to each other and making crane sounds.

Watching them, the girl and I both smiled.

"Your sister's cute," said the girl.

"Your brother is too. I'm Shoshana," I said again.

She looked at me closely. "Nani."

"Your bag," I said. "It's beautiful. You made it your own self?"

"Yes."

"I love those cranes! We saw them fly over!"

"We did too."

"It was so . . ." I couldn't think of the right English words. "I wanted to fly too," I said intently.

Papa's hand clapped down on my shoulder. "Ready, Shoshana?" he asked.

The girl immediately turned away and grabbed her brother as he circled past.

"Bye!" I called.

Pearlie hugged Papa's leg. "Papa, that girl has crane on her bag!"

"She did, Papa. It was beautiful."

"I noticed it too," Papa said. "Very striking. That's the Dakota beadwork Anshel was telling you about when you first came."

"It must take so long to learn," I said wistfully. "I wish I could do it."

So many tiny stitches. And how did she hold the minuscule beads in place? How long it must have taken her, stitching patiently at night by the fire, thinking of cranes all the while.

I remembered how I had felt when they flew overhead, crane after crane after crane, all together, untamed, indomitable, their glorious, fierce cries in the cold sky.

Nani loved this prairie just the way I did. Even more, I figured, because she had been here longer. I could see that love in her art. When the cranes flew over, Nani must have looked up at the same time I did, and, just as I had, felt their pull, their majesty, their power.

She still had the sky. But the land, which had been her people's for always, had been stolen away.

Twenty-One

"Sorry you weren't here last week, Libke!" Evie said on Monday, as we all hurried into the schoolhouse and hung up our wraps. "Hey, that ribbon looks so pretty on you! Look at what we did when you were home feeling poorly." She pulled down some of the cutouts that had been drying on the second shelf. "We started making Christmas decorations! See the fluffy Santa beards? That was me and Shoshana! We collected milkweed!"

I knew Libke didn't understand most of what Evie was talking about. I hoped the word *Christmas* hadn't registered. I glanced at my sister uneasily.

"Dank you kindly gif me ribbon, Evie," Libke said, the way she had practiced with me on the walk to school. She touched it softly with her finger. "So, so pretty!"

"Sure! I outgrew the dress it went with, did Shoshana tell you? It looks great with your gray dress. Anyway, we're going to make snowflakes next time we stay indoors at recess, for more Christmas decorations. You can help! And then we can start putting everything up around the room."

"Snow . . . ?" asked Libke.

"We cut paper into pretty patterns. Like flakes of snow, the tiny bits that come down from the sky?" Evie lifted her hands over her head and wiggled her fingers downward.

Libke nodded. "Snow-flake," she repeated carefully.

"Yes. But we make them bigger. We cut them out of paper. I love how every pattern comes out different. 'Specially because some of mine come out just dreadful, but then I just toss them in the stove and try a new one! As long as Miss Jansen keeps letting us use paper, it's no problem. And she's a real softie when it comes to Christmas. She loves it! We do a Christmas recital every year."

"Oh, you think I'm a softie, do you, Miss Evie Pedersen?" asked Miss Jansen, laughing. She had come up behind Evie to ring the school bell, but we hadn't heard her because of all the noise in the schoolroom. "We'll see if I'm a softie when it comes to your spelling!"

"Not about spelling! About Christmas, I said!" protested Evie. "That's a good thing to be a softie about! Everybody loves Christmas! And getting ready for it is the best part. I'm making my Mama a striped scarf, yellow and green, and the only thing I'm stuck on is what to make for mean old Frances, but I have to make her something . . ."

"Hush now, Evie, you chatterbox!" said Miss Jansen fondly, ringing the bell. "You can talk more with your friends at recess."

"Shoshana, you didn't!" Libke whispered to me in Yiddish, looking troubled, as we slid into our desk. "You made Christmas decorations?"

"No! I didn't really *make* them! I just collected the milkweed. Evie wanted me to! Evie's my friend."

"Evie's nice," Libke agreed. "It was so kind of her to give me the ribbon. Though I still think we should share it." Libke touched the dark-blue velvet bow caressingly with two fingers. "It's so soft!"

"No, thanks," I said again. "A ribbon around my throat would make me feel choked."

"But Shoshana, you should have explained to Evie. Jews don't make Christmas decorations. Mama and Papa wouldn't like it. You know they wouldn't."

"But paper snowflakes?" I protested. "That's what the girls are doing next. There's nothing wrong with making snowflakes, surely? Snow is just part of winter, not Christmas."

"Snowflakes are all right, I suppose," said Libke doubtfully. "But, Shoshana, we have to remember who we are."

But what if the people here didn't like us the way we were? I thought. What if being who we were made things terribly hard and lonesome? Or worse?

What if showing everyone who you were all the time was downright dangerous?

It was frightening, being far away from other Jews. What if people here turned against us for being Jewish, the way they had in the old country?

Papa had said there were no gangs here to go after us, no shouting peasants with clubs and flaming torches, no soldiers, no Cossacks, to join in the attacks. And some of our neighbors, like the Pedersens, had been generous and kind.

But things could change. Was it wrong that I didn't want to feel different all the time? That I didn't want to feel afraid, somewhere far in the back of my mind, every single day?

"Come to order, class," Miss Jansen said, and I looked up. The sky had brightened. Light slanted through the window, glinting off the glass of the schoolroom clock. It wouldn't be indoor recess today. I was glad to put off the awkwardness of the Christmas decorations as long as possible.

I squinted at my arithmetic problems. The sun glared blindingly on my slate.

I loved my family. Now that we had made the dugout ours, I even loved our strange little underground American house. With my baby sisters running around, and the smells of Mama's cooking, with Zissel and Berchik curled by the fire, with our clean white walls and a mezuzah to touch when we went in and out, our dugout and our claim were starting to feel like home.

But home wasn't just a piece of land. It wasn't just one family, all alone. It was bigger than that. It was being connected with the people around you, too. Home was where you had friends—friends at school, neighbors to help you get by. And none of our nearby neighbors or schoolmates here in America were Jews. The Kantors and the other Jewish families Papa and Anshel had celebrated the High Holidays with were miles off.

To the people living nearby to us, Jews were strange. Sinful, even. Without meaning to do it, Evie had let me know a little about what people were saying about my family.

Maybe we should try to blend in a little more, just to get along. To keep bad things from happening.

Was it wrong for me to want to blend in? If you could be the hawk or the prairie dog, who would choose to be the prairie dog? Even if most of the time you got to run around on the prairie, sitting on your haunches, chittering to your friends, popping in and out of holes, you never knew when a hawk with deadly claws was going to plunge down on you out of the deep blue of the sky.

I stole a glance at Libke, bent studiously over her sums. I couldn't remember ever having disagreed with my big sister about anything so important before. But I believed Libke was wrong about this. I believed we should try to fit in.

Twenty-Two

"For the Christmas recital, we'll make a stage on the teacher's platform," Miss Jansen explained the next day. "I'll need some strong scholars to carry my desk off to the side. All of you will say your pieces or sing your songs up there. Wear your nicest clothes! Your families are invited. Be sure you learn your pieces well. I want to be proud of every one of you. Now, let's rise and sing 'America the Beautiful.'"

Libke and I hummed along until we came to "Amer—eeka, Amer—eeka!" which I belted out. Libke sang those words out too, but not as loudly.

The sky darkened throughout the morning. By lunchtime you could tell for sure that winter was here. Tiny bits of ice spat down from the sky, clicking against the windows.

"Paper snowflake weather!" called Evie joyfully as we got out our lunches and spread them on our desks. "Eat fast, everyone, so we have time to make lots!"

The gray sky was bleak, but Nils had brought in a big pile of fuel for the stove in the morning, so the schoolhouse was warm and cozy.

Or it would have been if Clive and Mac and Fred hadn't been at school that day. But they were. And they came back in before the noon hour was over.

Clive walked toward our group, pretending to warm his hands at the stove. He leaned over Libke. She shrank against me.

I jumped up and pushed between Libke and Clive. "Stay away from her!" I said, clenching my fists.

"Ooh, look, this little Yid's a fighter!" Clive laughed. "I was just going to compliment your sister on her new ribbon. It's real nice." He grinned at Mac and Fred. "Makes me want to do this . . ." He held out his hand, pretending to dangle a ribbon from it, then opened it up as if he were letting the ribbon fall. He fisted his hands between his legs and made a long, drawn-out peeing sound. "Pssssssss! Pee-yew! Enjoy your ribbon, Yids!"

"Oh, hush up, Clive Huber," said Evie half-heartedly. "It was *my* ribbon. I gave it to Libke. It's perfectly clean. You keep your hands off."

I glared at Clive. "Libke not smell bad! YOU smell bad!"

Clive flicked at my hair. I flinched and took a step back. Clive swaggered off.

"See!" I said to the others, sitting down again. "That proves! Clive drop Libke's ribbon in the privy! We can tell Miss Jansen."

"Don't, Shoshana," Libke whispered in Yiddish. She almost sounded angry. "*Zay azoy gut*, just *please* don't make a big fuss! It makes more trouble. I want to forget it ever happened."

"He's only showing off," said Irene. "He does that kind of thing to me, when Pa's not around. It doesn't mean he threw the ribbon in the privy. It isn't enough proof to make Miss Jansen take notice."

"He likes the attention," said Grace. "Ignore him. Come on, let's make snowflakes."

"You all gobble your dinners like harvest hands!" Irene said, daintily dabbing at her lips. "My Mama says eating slowly is better for the digestion. So are we going to do a song for the Christmas recital?"

"Libke, you have such a pretty voice," Grace said. "You'll sing with us, won't you?"

"Let's make snowflakes," Evie said, jumping up and fetching the paper and scissors. "We can figure all that out later. You fold your paper like this. Now, take the scissors and cut out shapes. Then we'll open them up and see what they look like."

"Ta-da!" said Grace, opening hers. "Oops! I must have folded my paper wrong."

"So what song should we do?" Irene asked. "Grace, I need the scissors."

Grace passed her a pair. "Remember how last year me and you, Evie, wanted to do 'Silent Night' and Milly and Irene wanted 'Little Town of Bethlehem'?" she said. "Irene, you and Milly *promised* we could do 'Silent Night' this year."

"That's fine," said Irene. "I don't care. Just so long as I don't have to memorize a long poem. I hate that." She unfolded her snowflake. "Now that's a beautiful one!" she said. "See how tiny the cuts are? The trick is to cut with just the very points of the scissors."

"All right by me," Milly said. "If Miss Jansen will let me dress up as Mary and sit in front while you sing. Can we use your doll, Irene? For the Baby Jesus?"

"Well . . ." said Irene. "Maybe a cloth doll would be better. Softer. More like a real baby."

"We can use Baby Helen," said Evie. "So long as nobody minds that she's a girl."

"All of our dolls are girls," said Irene. "My Priscilla certainly is, with her golden curls." She tossed her own long hair back over her shoulder. "With rag dolls, you can't really tell the difference."

Evie rolled her eyes at Grace and Milly. "We can tell!" she said to Irene.

I snipped at my paper. It was hard to cut holes that weren't along the fold of the paper, but I tried a few. I stole a glance at Libke. I hoped she was thinking about paper snowflakes, not about the songs the girls were talking about. But she'd understood more than I'd thought.

"'Silent Night,'" Libke said slowly. "Song you will sing. This is Christmas song?"

"A Christmas carol? Yes," said Grace.

"About Jesus?" Libke asked.

"Sure!" said Milly. "It's about the night baby Jesus was born. In a stable, surrounded by horses and oxen and other animals. That's why I want to dress up like Mary holding baby Jesus."

"Think of the animals, Libke!" I said pleadingly. "Goats and sheep and horses! A little goat with brown feet, like the one you tell Tsivia and Pearlie stories about! Maybe there was even a cat like Zissel, to keep down the rats in the stable!"

Libke shook her head. She stood up, still holding her folded piece of paper.

"No," she said loudly and firmly, in English. "We cannot. Shoshana, you know, this we cannot. Jews cannot sing Jesus song."

Twenty-Three

Libke strode to the schoolroom stove, opened the door, letting out a blast of heat, and tossed in her folded piece of paper.

I jumped up and ran after her. "Libke! That's so wasteful!" I cried in Yiddish. "Don't you even want to see what your snowflake looks like?"

I pried open the stove door and grabbed the poker, but her snowflake was already licked by flames. It unfolded itself as I watched, glowed red around each lacy, outlined hole for a moment, then blackened and shriveled up.

"It was so pretty!" I lamented. "It would have looked wonderful on a window. You could have brought it home for Tsivia and Pearlie. Libke, why did you do that?"

Libke closed the door of the stove and drew me into the cloakroom, where she burst out in Yiddish. "We can't sing a song about Jesus, Shoshana. You know we can't."

"It's just singing!" I protested.

"Would you sing that song in front of Mama and Papa? All the families are invited to the Christmas recital, Miss Jansen said."

I felt my face going hot. "Mama and Papa don't know about it yet," I muttered. "We wouldn't have to tell them."

"Not tell Mama and Papa? Not invite our family? Shoshana! What are you saying?"

"Well, you said it too. They would be upset if they understood what the song was about. Papa would understand the English words, even if Mama wouldn't."

"We don't have to sing a Christmas song with the other girls. Miss Jansen said we could recite a poem. Maybe we could even say a poem in Yiddish together, since we're new."

"I am *not* saying a poem in Yiddish in front of all the kids and all the parents, Libke! I can talk some English now. So can you."

"Then we could say an easy English poem. I think I can learn one, if you help me. Mama and Papa would be proud."

"But just think," I moaned. "If we invite our family, Mama would wear her *shtern-tikhl*, you know she would! Don't you want to have friends here? Everyone would think we looked so foreign, so Jewish. They'd laugh at us behind our backs. It would be humiliating, Libke!"

Before I saw it coming, Libke's hand burned across my face. I held my hand to my cheek, stunned. My gentle sister, who eased the tangles out of my curls. She'd never hurt me before—never, ever!

"Shoshana! They're our parents! They've loved us, cared for us, worked for us, night and day. Honor your father and mother, remember? That's the worst thing I've ever heard you say!"

Libke's eyes blazed at me, miserable and fierce, like the paper snowflake blackening in the stove. "Are you ashamed I'm your sister, too? How could you, Shoshana? Being ashamed of your people is like being ashamed of yourself!"

Libke walked out of the cloakroom. I followed her, my cheek smarting. Libke didn't go back to our desk, where the other girls were cutting snowflakes. She stood uncertainly, looking around, then walked to where little Betsy and Emily were sitting. After a few minutes, Nils walked over to her.

My eyes were tearing. It hadn't been a hard slap. But my sister. My best friend. I couldn't believe she had hit me.

"Why'd she get mad at you?" Milly demanded when I sat down. "She's usually so nice."

"Don't be nosy, Milly," Evie said. "Sisters fight sometimes. Big sisters can be bossy. Believe me, I know."

"Libke not want to sing 'Silent Night,'" I muttered, with my head down.

Grace sighed. "Oh, too bad! And she has such an angel voice!"

"That's all right," said Evie. "You'll still sing with us, won't you?"

Libke didn't want anything to do with me now. She had made that very clear. I only hesitated for a moment. "Yes."

"Oh, good. Here, make another snowflake." Evie pushed a piece of paper and some scissors over to me. "You've hardly had a chance to do any. Isn't it fun? I look forward to Christmastime just for making snowflakes and cookies! And for the snow, real snow! Well, at least the first few times, I love it, when it isn't a blizzard. It's so clean and pretty. Sometimes I eat it! Did you ever try that? It's especially nice when you have some molasses and brown sugar warming, or your Ma does, and you run in with fresh snow and pour molasses on it. Yum! The best taste ever, and I mean ever!"

"Have you tried hot maple syrup on snow?" Milly asked eagerly. "My cousins in Boston sent us some maple syrup one year. It's even better than molasses!"

I snipped at my snowflake, letting the other girls' voices drift over me. I peeked at Libke. She and Nils had their heads bent together over a book.

Irene held a snowflake up for us to admire. "Look! That's the best snowflake yet!" she crowed. "Don't you girls think so?"

"I like mine," said Evie.

"Oh, come on, Evie! Isn't mine the best?" she asked the rest of us. "With all the tiny, delicate holes in it?"

"It's pretty," I said. "All are pretty. Will look so nice on the window."

I could tell that wasn't enough praise for Irene. She stood up and held her snowflake against the pane of glass next to us. Through the holes in the paper, we saw the white and gray of the sky. She peeled one of the other girls' snowflakes off the glass, put hers in the center, and pasted it there, then looked at it admiringly. Grace and Milly rolled their eyes at each other.

"You know," Irene said, coming back to the desks. "Maybe Libke is right. I mean, maybe Yids shouldn't sing a Christian hymn."

"Irene!" said Evie. "That's not a nice word."

"It isn't?" said Irene. "That's what my Pa calls them. Don't get your feelings hurt over it, Shoshana. I just think maybe *Jews* shouldn't sing one of our hymns."

"Of course she can sing with us!" Evie insisted. "Jesus was a Jew, you know."

"He was? He turned into a Christian later, though, right?" said Grace.

"And then the Jews killed him," said Irene confidently.

"No! The Jews did not!" I knew that wasn't true. Mama had told me long ago, back in our village, when the peasants were saying the same thing. "The Romans killed Jesus. Jews not in charge! Jews never, not ever, kill people . . ."

I held my fingers up in a plus shape, not knowing the word.

"On a cross you mean?" asked Evie.

"Yes. Jews never! This is not a true thing Christians say, that Jews kill Jesus."

The other girls glanced at each other. "I'm very sorry," said Irene, not sounding sorry at all, "but I do believe you are wrong about that. We definitely learned that in Sunday school. The Jews killed Jesus. His blood is on their hands."

My face got hot. They were wrong. I knew they were wrong.

"It was a really long time ago, though," Milly said, soothingly. "We don't think it's your fault or anything."

179

"And you don't *seem* very Jewish, Shoshana," Grace said.

Grace looked at me expectantly. So did the other girls.

I knew what she wanted me to say. Grace and Milly and Irene were all looking at me, waiting. Even Evie looked expectant. I didn't want to say it. But it seemed as if somebody else was making my lips move. "Thanks," I muttered. My face felt stiff.

"You're right, she doesn't, really," said Milly. "Neither does Anshel. You don't have those Jewish noses!" She crumpled a discarded paper snowflake and held it over her own snub nose. The light from the schoolroom fire cast a grotesque shadow onto the wall beside her. The other girls laughed.

I felt myself laughing weakly. My cheeks were tight. My heart throbbed as if it were going to burst. My eyes burned. I needed to swallow, but for a moment I couldn't.

"And any time you want to become a Christian, you can, Shoshana," Evie said kindly. "It isn't your fault, what family you were born into. My mother says you just have to accept Jesus Christ as your savior. And then you'll be washed clean of all sin."

I couldn't think of any words to say, not any at all. I bent my head and concentrated on my snowflake, snipping tiny little triangles along the fold.

Twenty-Four

Libke sat turned away from me all afternoon, even though I bumped her once with my elbow, pretending it was an accident, trying to get her to talk to me. But she just inched away.

After school, I lingered in the cloakroom. Maybe Libke would come over and tell me she was sorry for slapping me and then we would walk home together, the way we always did.

But Libke grabbed her shawl without glancing in my direction and hurried out. When I looked out the schoolroom door, I saw that Nils was walking with her. She had her head turned toward him, smiling.

How could Libke be happy? She hadn't even taken our lunch pail and milk bottles, and it was her turn to carry them. Maybe I should just leave them here. But what would we carry our lunch in tomorrow, if I did? I grabbed the lunch pail angrily, slamming the bottles in it against each other, and left the cloakroom.

"Have a good evening, Shoshana," Miss Jansen said to me from her desk.

"Thank you, Miss Jansen," I said automatically. "Goodbye."

All the other children were gone. I dawdled around the schoolyard, giving Libke and Nils time to get far ahead of me, not wanting to run into them on the way home. Miss Jansen peered at me once from the window, but when I caught her eye, she just smiled and returned to her desk. She must be preparing tomorrow's lessons. Knowing she was in there made me feel a tiny bit less alone.

When I was sure Libke and Nils were far ahead, I started toward home.

The gray sky hung low, but the wind had died down during the course of the afternoon. The frost on the grass, so crunchy under my feet on the way to school, had completely melted, leaving damp patches here and there. I walked alone under the huge sky. The wind was behind me, whipping bits of hair in my face, whipping my skirt ahead, shoving me forward. I wondered if Libke was too busy laughing with Nils to remember me at all.

"Zissel!" I called, wishing my cat would come pouncing out of the grass and run along with me. But I only heard the wind and the cries of birds. Without Libke, I suddenly felt too alone on the enormous prairie. Usually it felt stark but glorious, vast and free. Today there was something looming about the gray sky, something too forlorn, too quiet. I started to hurry, wishing I were in our warm dugout already, eating a piece of bread at the rough table, telling Mama what we'd learned at school before going out to milk Royt and check for eggs in the chicken coop.

I was getting close to home when I smelled something that shouldn't have been there. Smoke from a campfire mixed with the dirty, low-hanging smell of cigarettes. And then I heard voices.

"There she is. The little Yid."

"By herself?"

"Yeah, just the loudmouth!"

Clive, Fred, and Mac came up out of a gully. They stood on the path looking at me.

"Hey there, Ugly!" jeered Clive. "Hi, Jew girl!"

Just ignore them, Evie had said, Grace had said, Libke had said. *Pretend you don't hear.*

But now I was all alone. Surrounded by empty prairie. And there were three of them.

Fred drew on his cigarette, dropped it on the path, and ground it into the dirt with his foot.

"We're talking to you, Yid," he said. "You too good to talk to us? Answer when you're spoken to."

I lifted my chin, trying to look bored and unconcerned. My mouth felt sticky. My hands were cold. I pulled them under my shawl.

"Did you like the picture I drew?" called Mac.

He took a casual step toward me. The others followed, blotting out the sky. Mac had a huge, barrel-shaped chest. Fred's arms were wiry, with knotted ropes of muscle. Clive was tall and broad-shouldered, as big as Papa almost. My heart thudded.

"Why'd you tear it up, Yid?" Clive asked. "You hurt Mac's feelings!"

"Boo-hoo!" wailed Mac. "Didn't I draw your horns right?"

I couldn't keep silent any longer. "Jews don't have horns!" I shouted. "That's poopycock! Stupid! Only animals have horns." I darted off the path, trying to get around them.

I saw a blur of grins, and my left arm was yanked backwards. Mac's foul breath was close to my face. "What did you say? *Poopy*?" He laughed raucously. "When you going to learn English, Jew girl?"

I wrenched my arm away. "Jews don't have horns!" I shouted. "Only animals!"

"Let's see!" Mac grabbed me again, pinning my wrists behind my back. "Check now, Fred!"

Clive and Fred closed in on me, shoving their filthy hands through my hair. For a moment I couldn't breathe. "Get off!" I tried to shout, but my voice stuck in my throat.

"Here's one," shouted Clive, shoving his hand down hard on my skull.

"No way! She really has them? That's disgusting!"

Fred grabbed at the spot where Clive's hand had been. "Here? Where's the other one? You're sly! Hiding them! Pretending to be a normal girl!"

I gasped for air. This time my yell blasted out like a train whistle. "Get off me! Help! Help! Berchik! Come!" I kicked as hard as I could.

"Ow!" Clive hopped on one foot. "Nasty kike!"

"Hold her, Clive," shouted Mac. "I wanna feel it."

Clive squeezed my shoulders back viciously. Mac's hand slammed down on the same spot on my head. "Yeah, that *is* one! Repulsive! You filthy Yid!"

A hand passed by my face and I jerked my chin forward and bit into it as hard as I could.

Someone yelled. Then I heard a rush in the shrubbery, a fierce yowling snarl, and shouts. I twisted one of my wrists free, turned, and dug my nails into Clive's beefy hand on my other wrist, twisting and writhing. "Let me go!"

More shrieks and yells came from nearby, yells of pain, of rage.

"What is it?" Clive shouted.

"A goddamn cat!"

I caught a glimpse of Zissel, a black-and-white blur, sinking her teeth into Fred's leg. He screamed, shaking her off, and she pounced on his other leg, clawing and biting. He kicked and danced away, cursing.

"The Yid's cat!" Mac threw his jacket over Zissel and snatched her up in a writhing bundle.

"Throw it in the fire!"

I saw again the Cossacks' boots, the cruel stick. The wailing cat streaking through the village with a blackened tail.

Fury and strength flooded through me. I wrenched myself away from Clive and ran toward Mac, dizzy. "No! Zissel!" I cried.

A black-and-white shape flew through the air toward the campfire. Zissel screamed.

Everything blurred. I grabbed Zissel and flung her away from the fire. Heat seared my hands. Zissel flipped onto her feet, yowled and snarled at them, then ran toward home.

"Run, Zissel!" My feet thudded after her, running as fast as I could. My chest ached. Zissel bounded ahead of me, looping back, howling. The boys' voices were behind me, then fainter and farther behind. I saw our dugout, swelling up from the ground, and the chimney pipe.

In there?

No.

Libke, Mama, too many questions.

I ran to the barn and through the door.

Was Zissel burned? She didn't seem to be, though she streaked around the barn, distraught and wailing.

I burrowed into a pile of hay and sobbed.

I cried for a long time. I felt filthy all over.

The sweet-smelling hay surrounded me now, and I burrowed into it. Its scratchiness felt good, as if it could clean me.

One of my hands throbbed, and I cradled it.

Why had they done that? Was there something wrong about me?

Was it because I'd tried to be like the other girls?

One of the boys had said something like that. That I was pretending.

But I wasn't! I just wanted friends! I wanted to fit in.

Would Libke say it was my fault too?

I worked my fingers through my curls and gently touched the sore spot on my skull where Clive had slammed his hand. I winced.

It wasn't a horn, was it? It was just the back bump of my skull. I felt around, and I had one just like it on the other side. Didn't everybody have that? I was pretty sure they did.

But Clive and Fred and Mac had called me "Yid" and grabbed at my head, disgusted by me. As if I were nothing. As if I were dirt. As if I were less than nothing.

Clive and Fred and Mac might tease the other girls, but they would never do that to someone like Irene or Milly.

Was North Dakota going to be like when we lived in Ukraine? Were we going to have to leave here too?

Why did so many people think there was something wrong with being Jewish?

Even trying to be like the others didn't keep the kids at school from thinking that I was different. Strange. Wrong.

I couldn't tell Evie and the other girls what Clive and those other boys had done to me. I couldn't even tell Mama. I felt too confused, too ashamed. Libke? But Libke didn't act like my sister anymore.

I sobbed.

Zissel pushed up against me, nosing my arm insistently until I moved it and let her put her nose against my cheek.

I held her close. "Are you hurt, little Zissel?" I asked.

She meowed and licked at her right hind paw where Fred had kicked her. I felt it gently. Nothing seemed broken. Zissel nosed my hand, then went back to licking her paw.

At least I had Zissel. Brave Zissel. Fierce Zissel. Hardly more than a kitten and she had attacked three nearly grown men. Distracted them so I could get away.

I stayed in the barn for a long time, at first with Zissel and then, when she wiggled away after a while, all by myself, my face pressed against the hay.

Twenty-Five

At dinner, I spooned up my soup slowly. My shoulders and wrists ached. My right hand throbbed. The skin on my scalp felt raw.

"More soup, *mamele*?" Mama asked me gently. "You were a long time in the barn doing your chores today. What happened to your wrist? Did you burn yourself? Is that a bruise? Did something happen at school?"

I looked at my wrist, noticed a red-and-purple mark, and pulled down my sleeve. "I'm fine," I said. I wasn't hungry.

When we washed the dishes, Libke stopped suddenly. "The lunch pail! It was my turn to carry it home, but I forgot. Did you bring it?"

I was dizzy and aching, and the people around me felt far away. "No," I said, slowly. I must have dropped it near the gully. "I don't have it."

"Girls!" Mama said in exasperation. "Well, you'll have to carry your lunch in a bundle tomorrow."

"Sorry, Mama," said Libke, goody-goody, perfect Libke. "I won't forget again."

"Can Berchik walk to school with us tomorrow?" I asked, after I finished drying the dishes.

Anshel looked at me intently. "Is somebody bothering you, Shoshi?"

I dropped my eyes.

"She's just mad because I wouldn't walk home with her today," Libke said impatiently.

Anshel studied me. "Sure, you can take him," he said. "Berchik used to go to school with me. He knows how to find shelter in the day and then come bounding up as soon as school's out."

"*A dank*, Anshel," I said.

"I need to check on Royt," Anshel said. "I think her hoof is sore. Come with me, Shoshi? She likes you."

I nodded numbly, glad to get out of the too-close dugout.

"Is everything all right?" he asked, when we were in the barn. "Something happened, didn't it? I know what those kids at school are like."

I looked at him miserably, but I couldn't speak.

My big brother patted my shoulder. I winced. "Oh, Shoshi," he said softly. "I'm sorry. Berchik will keep you and Libke safe now. I should have sent him with you before. You'll tell me what happened when you're ready?"

I nodded. My throat swelled painfully, and I was struggling not to cry.

I woke up late, aching all over. Libke was already braiding her hair. I always did that for her so that it would hang straight down her back. Now it hung, tight and neat, but twisting slightly where she had pulled it over her shoulder to finish it.

Why hadn't she waited for me? I shook my own hair free from its loose nighttime braid. Across the room, Pearlie was stamping out a rhythm while Mama tried to put on her clothes.

"Come here, Tsivia," Libke called. "I'll button up your dress."

"What about my hair, Libke?" I asked. "Aren't you going to do it?"

"Do it yourself."

I frowned, reached for the comb, and started tugging it through my curls, sitting on the edge of our new bed in a heap of quilts and feather beds. Even in a braid, my hair got so snarled overnight. Libke and I always helped each other before we dressed the twins. The little ones didn't have to get ready for school. There wasn't any hurry for them.

I yanked the comb impatiently and it caught on a snarl, tugging on the sore part of my scalp. "Ow!" I cried.

"Don't make such a fuss," Libke said over her shoulder. "Just start at the bottom and go at it slowly. You're old enough to comb out your own hair."

"Tsivia comb own hair!" my little sister said smugly, looking at Libke for approval and banging Mama's comb energetically against her scalp.

"Yours is straight," I muttered. "Try combing *kutsherave hor* like mine and Pearlie's! Anyone can comb hair like yours." She wasn't really combing it anyway.

"Not anyone who is three," Libke said. "Very good, Tsivia."

Tsivia beamed and scampered off to join Mama and Pearlie, who were getting ready to go out to the barn.

"If you're so ashamed of our family," Libke said as soon as the dugout door closed behind them, "then why don't you get your new best friend, E-vie"—she drew out her name in a mocking sing-songy way—"to comb your hair? I'm sure you wouldn't want your Jewish sister combing it, talking to you in Yiddish!"

"That's stupid!" I said angrily. "I never said we couldn't talk Yiddish at home. And anyway, you were talking English with Nils yesterday, weren't you? He doesn't speak Yiddish. So why can't you try talking it more with Evie and the others?"

Libke sighed as if I were just too stupid to talk to, as if I didn't understand anything at all. She got up from the bed.

"Wait, your braid is twisted," I said. I reached out to straighten it, but just as my fist closed on her hair, she pulled away from me.

"Ow! Let go! You're pulling my hair now?" She glared at me. "My braid is fine. And it's easy to talk to Nils, because he's nice to me! He doesn't fit in either, with his bad foot. He remembers when he couldn't speak English, and he doesn't laugh when I make mistakes or sound funny."

"I wasn't pulling! I was just trying to untwist it! And I never said I was ashamed of you! I didn't mean that! My friends don't laugh at you!" I paused, because that wasn't entirely true. I was certain Evie wouldn't, but I had heard Milly do it, and I wasn't at all sure about the others. "It's just," I was getting all confused. "It's just . . . we need to try! We don't want people thinking we're different all the time!"

"Right," Libke said flatly. "That's what I said. You don't want to be like the rest of us. You don't want to be part of our family."

"I never said that!"

"You might as well have!" Libke said. "I know that's what you mean. I'm all alone here too! I miss home! I miss our village. I miss Bela and Rivka most of all! Evie's your friend, but I don't have any friends my age here, except Nils. I can't learn English as fast as you. And now you say not to talk Yiddish at school. Or just to whisper if I absolutely have to, because you're so ashamed! You don't want to be my sister anymore!"

"I do! I didn't say that! You're the one who slapped *me*!" A confusion of misery and hurt swirled through me. I couldn't find the words to make her understand, to pull Libke back to me. My heart felt swollen. It was all I could do not to cry. Libke and I never fought like this. And now no matter what I said, she got angrier and angrier, further and further away. What if she never loved me again? How could this have happened?

For the first mile or so, as we walked to school over the snow-dusted prairie, under a leaden sky, Libke didn't say a single word.

As we got near the gully where those boys had grabbed me, my heart started pounding wildly in my chest. I'd been thinking so much about Libke being mad that I'd forgotten I'd have to walk right by it. My legs wobbled. I slowed down. Suddenly, I felt as if I couldn't go forward. My breath came fast. Libke walked on ahead. I watched her twisted braid bouncing on her plaid shawl.

"Hey, there's our lunch pail!" Libke picked it up and glared at me. "You dropped it? Did you fall here or something? Is that how you got that bruise?"

I shrugged. At first I couldn't speak, but then I called after her. "Could you come back here just for a minute, Libke? *Zay azoy gut*? Please?"

I desperately needed her. I needed to be able to tell her everything. I needed to grab her hand and run past that awful spot. I needed Libke to tell me that I was safe now.

"Libke?" I called again. "*Zay azoy gut*, sister? Please? It's really important."

"What?" she yelled. "Why are you just standing there? Hurry up. We're going to be tardy!"

Libke wouldn't come back. She didn't care about me anymore. I squinted my eyes until I could see only a blur of steel-gray grasses and somber sky. I ran as fast as I could toward Libke and Berchik, my feet thumping the ground, jarring me, my breath coming short and quick and hard. As I was almost up to them, I slipped and fell, dropping my books and banging my knee against the frozen ground.

Berchik panted happily back to me. But Libke hurried on. She seemed to want to stay as far away from me as possible. I put my hand in Berchik's fur. His back was solid and strong. My heart slowly stopped thudding. With Berchik, I would be safe. He was such a good dog.

I picked up my books, and found a stick. "Hey, Berchik!" I called. I waved it in front of him. "Fetch!" I sent it sailing down the path, whisking above Libke's head. She turned and frowned, opened her mouth as if she were going to say something, then snapped it closed again.

"Good boy, good boy!" I told Berchik loudly as he came bounding back. "Such a good boy! You're my friend, aren't you? Yes, you are!" I rubbed his neck. "Give me the stick. Let go, Berchik! Fetch!" This time I sent the stick sailing past Libke's ear.

Libke turned around again as Berchik bounded gleefully past her. "You keep that stick away from me, Shoshana," she said through gritted teeth. "There's a whole prairie. You can throw it in absolutely any other direction!"

Libke ran down the edge of the ridge, heading for the school, then tore across the flat land toward the schoolhouse. I ran after her down the ridge, then collapsed at the bottom. Berchik sat down next to me, panting, his tongue hanging out.

My throat hurt so much that I could hardly swallow. I buried my face against Berchik's fur. My head ached. My hand felt numb. My right knee throbbed where it had just hit the ground. I hurt all over. I didn't want to go on to school where those boys would be, especially with Libke being so mean.

But I didn't want to go home either. Mama would ask lots of questions. I couldn't have peace anywhere.

I watched the small figure of Miss Jansen come out onto the schoolhouse steps and ring the bell. The scholars lined up, girls in one line and boys in the other. I thought Libke glanced my way, but I couldn't tell for sure. Her dress blended with the steel gray of the grass.

Why had Libke said those awful things? That I didn't want to be her sister? That I didn't want to be part of my family anymore?

She was wrong! I did want to be part of my family! Libke was the one who had slapped *me*. She was the one who wouldn't walk back even a little way so I wouldn't have to go past the gully by myself. Even though I'd begged her!

It was so cruel of her not to walk back a few steps, when I needed her to. She should have come. Even though she didn't know what had happened to me there, she must have heard the misery in my voice.

Once Libke had seemed to understand everything about me. Now she didn't seem to understand anything at all.

Was Libke right that I didn't want to be Jewish anymore?

Those boys would never have done that to me if I hadn't been Jewish.

If we weren't Jews, absolutely everything would be easier. If we weren't Jews, we would get along better at school and with our neighbors. I *had* thought all that, deeply and silently, in my heart.

Why did so many other people, back when we lived in Ukraine and here, think that there was something so wrong about us?

Was it true that I was ashamed of who I was?

I was just trying to have friends! Everybody needed friends!

But I knew now, after what Clive and Mac and Fred had done to me, that trying to be like the others wouldn't work. The kids here would never forget that we were different.

So I didn't have any friends here, not real ones.

And now, even my own sister had turned away from me.

Twenty-Six

I rested my face against Berchik's warm body. Maybe I could sit there all day. After a while, though, the bitter cold of the ground seeped through my skirt. The wind began to whip fiercely around me. My hands grew numb.

I got up stiffly. "Stay nearby, Berchik. I'll be back as soon as I can."

I walked slowly across the stretch of prairie toward school.

The scholars all lifted their heads as I came in. Libke glanced at me and quickly looked back down at her desk.

"Tardy, Shoshana?" Miss Jansen sounded surprised. "You?" She opened her attendance book and put a mark in it.

After a while, I got up the courage to look around the schoolroom. The big boys weren't there. My breath came a little easier.

At noon, I sat with Evie and the other girls, huddled near the potbellied stove. Libke fetched our lunch pail from the cloakroom. She took some food out of it, shoved the pail toward me, and walked over to the little ones. Betsy immediately climbed onto Libke's lap and put her arms around her neck.

"Libke's still mad at you?" Evie asked, drawing a bundle out of her lunch pail. "Who wants to share my apricot rolls?"

"Apricot? Oh, right, you have those apricot trees!" Grace said. "I want one!"

"Those must take so much watering," Irene said. "I'm glad I don't have to do it!"

"Buckets and buckets," Evie agreed calmly, unwrapping the scrap of flowered cloth and arranging the rolls on it. "Sometimes Frances and I do it, but usually it's the field hands."

"Hey, what happened to your wrist, Shoshana?" Grace asked suddenly. "Is that a bruise?" All the girls stared at me.

"Does your Pa hit you?" asked Irene.

"Irene!" said Evie.

"What? Sorry, but she does have a bruise!"

"My Papa never hurt anybody! My family doesn't hurt people!"

"All right!" Irene tossed her head. "I was just asking! Some people's Pas *are* like that. Mostly with boys, though."

How dare she think something like that?

I glared at her. "You know you all say boys' horn picture just stupid? You say ignore it? You are wrong! You all say it is not big deal! It *is* big deal!" I jumped to my feet. "I change my mind," I blurted. "I don't want to sing the Christmas song." I ran into the cloakroom and buried my face in my shawl.

When I came back out, the other girls were standing on the teacher's platform looking at a songbook. Evie slipped into the desk next to me.

"What's the matter, Shoshana?" she whispered. "What happened?"

But I couldn't tell her. It was too shameful.

"Don't mind those boys, Shoshana, really. They're just stupid. Come on, I'll teach you 'Silent Night.' It isn't hard."

"No," I muttered, staring at the desk. In the corner, it looked as if someone had written on it once. The spot was scrubbed to a paler color than the rest of the wood. I rubbed at it with my finger.

"So are you going to learn a poem, then?" Evie persisted. "All by yourself? That's no fun!"

"We need you, Evie!" Irene called triumphantly from the front of the room. "I was right! It is 'love's pure light'!"

"In the *third* verse it is," muttered Grace. "Not in the second."

Evie sighed, patted my shoulder, and stood up. "It would be heaps more fun if you sang with us. Think it over."

I wasn't going to change my mind. I needed to find a poem.

Libke's reader would have shorter ones. I pulled it out of the desk and flipped through until I found a short poem called "Sunset." I muttered the first lines. "Now the sun is sinking / In the golden west."

I understood the words and I liked some of them. They reminded me of the sunset we saw that first night we rode out to the homestead in Papa's wagon. But my brain wasn't working. It just couldn't remember the English words. It was like a time once long ago when I had a high fever, and my words had come out all garbled, Libke had told me later. "Now the sun," was all I could remember before I had to look back at the page again. "Now the sun . . ."

From time to time, during the rest of the day, Evie looked at me worriedly, but she didn't say anything more.

After school, Berchik came racing up, his plumy tail waving. I knelt to hug him. With my face buried in his fur, I felt better than I had all day.

Libke and I didn't talk much on the way home, but we did walk side by side. When we passed the gully, my heart thudded again. *You're all right*, I told myself as I made myself march by. *Those boys aren't here. Berchik is here.*

Berchik, who had been running forward, looped back suddenly, as if he knew I needed him. I put my hand on his back, and felt my heart begin to slow down. "Good boy, Berchik," I told him.

Soon we saw a trail of smoke rising from our dugout.

"Libke," I said, "I decided I'm not going to sing the Christmas song with the other girls. I'm learning a poem instead."

Libke looked surprised. "Oh! That's good."

"The poem is in your reader. So I'll have to borrow it."

Libke frowned. "What if I need it, Shoshana? I have to do my schoolwork first. It takes me longer than it takes you."

"Well, you'll just have to let me use it sometimes, won't you? You're the one who wanted me to say a poem."

Without waiting for an answer, I ran toward the dugout.

Twenty-Seven

I spent most of my free time in the barn the next week, alone, practicing the fiddle. At school, I sat alone during recess forcing my head to learn the words to "Sunset" while Evie and the other girls rehearsed "Silent Night." I felt like a prairie dog huddled alone in an underground burrow, barely keeping warm in the bitter cold.

Friday was the first night of Chanukah. Mama set candles in the menorah on the deep dugout windowsill. We all gathered around and, as if from a distance, I watched Libke light the helper candle, the *shames*, and touch it to the first candle on the menorah, her fingers steady, the warm light illuminating her intent face. My sister is so beautiful, I thought. But it seemed like a thought coming from somewhere far away rather than a feeling inside me. It just seemed to float in and out of my head.

Two tiny points of honey-colored light danced, reflected in the windowpane set deep in the dugout wall. We turned to watch Mama as she said the Shabbos blessings and lit those candles too. On the table, the Shabbos candles glowed.

"Will you play the fiddle, Papa?" I asked.

"*Ach*, these old fingers of mine feel creaky," Papa groaned. "But I'll play a Chanukah song if you will all sing."

Papa's fingers flew, drawing such sweetness out of the old fiddle. Listening pulled me back to all the Chanukahs back at home, Malke knocking on our door with Dov right behind her, bringing hot, sweet jelly doughnuts bursting with cherry jam. A house full of neighbors. The men lifting a glass with Papa, gulping down the vodka, then slamming their glasses down in unison, gasping, "Ah!" I remembered crouching on the floor with Libke and small neighbor kids, seeing whose dreidl would stay up the longest. Anshel spinning his dreidl toward ours, trying to knock them over and then shrieking with joy when they collided and popped upward. The grown-ups' singing and laughter. The intense taste of cherries on my tongue. Looking up to watch the flames of the menorah dance. That all seemed so far away now. Here there were no neighbors next door. No one to celebrate our holidays with. Outside there was only space. Only night. Only wind.

When he had finished playing, Papa smiled at me. "I've been hearing you practice '*Oyfn Pripetshik*' in the barn. You're improving every day! Why don't you play it now and the rest of us can sing?"

Anshel grinned. "Yes, by now even I can almost recognize the tune in between the screeches," he said.

I was starting to remember how to tease my brother back. "Oh, shut up, Anshel!" I said. "Let's hear if you screech when you're singing! I remember how you used to, when your voice was breaking. *Oy-yoy-yoy!*"

Anshel laughed as I took the fiddle from Papa. I played as the others sang. Libke's voice soared over the others, sweet and true.

I glanced at Libke as I put the fiddle away. Would she be in a happy mood because of Chanukah?

But she was sitting on the floor with her back to me, playing dreidel with our little sisters. And something about the stiff way she was holding her back told me she didn't want me to join in the game.

Twenty-Eight

Although Libke was angry with me, she hadn't told our parents about the recital. I was glad. I'd given up on singing the Christmas carol, but I still didn't want my family to look foreign and speak Yiddish in front of everyone. What if Milly made a joke about Papa's nose and he heard it? I just couldn't bear that.

"How are we even going to get to the recital after supper on Wednesday if we don't tell Mama and Papa?" Libke murmured, frowning, as we did our hair on Monday morning. She said it softly enough so that Mama didn't hear. That was easy to do, because Tsivia had stuck a comb into Pearlie's hair and was yanking on it while Pearlie shrieked.

"I already asked Evie," I whispered. "She said they'll stop by to pick us up in the buggy. We can tell Mama it's a celebration for the last day of school before the vacation. She won't know that other parents will be there if we run out fast, so she and Papa won't mind not going."

"Don't you feel ashamed when you hear yourself saying things like that?" Libke hissed.

I did, actually. Sick in the pit of my stomach. But I'd feel even worse if our family came.

"Quiet, Pearlie," Mama said wearily. "*Ach*, I have such a splitting headache this morning!"

"Poor Mama," said Libke. "Do you want me to stay home so you can rest a little?"

Mama looked at her gratefully. "Such a good girl," she said. "*Gezunt zolstu zayn*! But I don't want you to miss a day of learning."

"We aren't working hard this week anyway, right Shoshana?" said Libke. "Because of the vacation coming. I won't miss much."

"Well, if you really think you won't fall behind. I do feel poorly. My head is acting up again."

"Lie down for a bit," Libke said soothingly. "I'll finish with breakfast."

"I didn't know your head still hurt, Mama," I said. "I could stay home too."

Libke rolled her eyes as if she didn't believe I could care about Mama too. Or maybe she didn't want me butting into her alone time with Mama.

"It only hurts every now and then, *mamele*. But I'm lucky to have such good daughters," Mama said, shading her eyes with her hand. "One of you staying home is enough. You go along to school, Shoshi. Wrap up warmly. It's going to be a very cold day."

It was snowing a bit—tiny, icy pellets—when I started out, so I called to Berchik to stay home. I couldn't bear the idea of snow falling on him while I was snug inside the schoolhouse.

On a day like this, I was sure Clive and his friends would find reasons to stay away from school, so I didn't need Berchik.

It snowed harder and faster as I walked. I fought my way through the wind, ducking my head against the tiny, sharp pellets of snow. When I pulled the schoolhouse door open, the wind tore it out of my hand, sending it thudding against the wall. I grabbed it with both hands and struggled against the wind to yank it closed behind me. Miss Jansen was standing by the window, looking out at the storm.

It was a few minutes past eight o'clock, but the schoolhouse was nearly empty of children. The back row, where the big boys always sat, was blessedly empty, as I had guessed it would be. So was the front row where the littlest ones perched. Their mothers must have decided the weather was too cold for them to make the long walk to school.

Irene warmed her hands at the stove. Clive must have dropped her off and headed back to his uncle's farm. Milly huddled close to Irene. Across the aisle, in the other spot closest to the stove, Evie sat sideways, knees near the fire. Behind her, Nils was shivering, his jacket tightly buttoned up.

"Hi, Shoshana!" Evie waved gaily. "You're one of the fearless ones too! Even my sister Frances stayed home. She has the sniffles, and Mama said the cold might make it go to her chest. Your sister too?"

Nils looked over at me. He was clearly listening.

"Not sick, but she stays home to take care of Mama and the little ones," I explained. "Mama's head aches."

"Oh, your poor Mama! But I'm glad you're here. Miss Jansen says we can come up close to the fire. It'll be so cozy! Likely no one else will be coming today."

I slipped into the desk next to Evie. It felt almost like a holiday. Miss Jansen opened the schoolhouse door to see if any more scholars were straggling toward us through the snow. A cold blast of wind tore around the room, making the fire flicker and then roar. I tugged my shawl tightly around me and slid against Evie's warmth.

Irene was talking gleefully about riding to school with Clive in the cutter instead of the buggy. I tried hard not to think of Clive, to drown out her words by dreaming of Domino instead, imagining how beautiful he must have looked this morning, black against the vast whiteness of the prairie, tossing his mane proudly, snow spraying out from under his hooves.

Miss Jansen came back to the stove and warmed her hands. "I think it's just going to be the five of you today, children," she said. "Shall we start with geography? Irene, please get out the globe."

"Aw, Miss Jansen," Evie coaxed. "Couldn't you maybe read to us? We should do something special."

"Well . . ." Miss Jansen looked at Evie's sweet, freckled face and then grinned. She especially liked Evie, I could tell. "I do have a brand-new book that my aunt just sent me all the way from Boston. It's called *A Little Princess*. It's about a girl named Sara Crewe and her troubles at school. A motherless girl about your age who travels all the way from her home in India to a boarding school in London. Sara's father leaves her there and goes back to India."

"Why?" gasped Milly. "How does she ever see him?"

"She doesn't. He has to work there," Miss Jansen explained. "So Sara stays alone in London at the school."

All alone! With her only family in another country! I felt a pain in my stomach. Poor Sara Crewe! My family might be embarrassing sometimes, but I was awfully glad they were here in North Dakota with me, all of them.

"Oh, please, read it to us, Miss Jansen!" Evie begged.

Miss Jansen took a brand-new blue book out of her desk. She opened it gently and smoothed the crisp pages. *"A Little Princess*, by Frances Hodgson Burnett," Miss Jansen announced: "Once on a dark winter's day, when the yellow fog hung so thick and heavy in the streets of London that the lamps were lighted and the shop windows blazed with gas as they do at night . . ."

Miss Jansen paused to glance out the window. The snow had stopped, and the sky was bright and clear. For once, the wind had gone utterly silent. She sighed in relief, and we all settled down to listen to the story as the fire crackled in the potbellied stove.

I liked Sara Crewe right away. But I didn't like Miss Minchin, the mean old teacher, not one bit. She told lies. And she wouldn't let Sara explain why she didn't need a beginning French book. "'I am afraid,' said Miss Minchin, with a slightly sour smile, 'that you have been a very spoiled little girl,'" Miss Jansen read, and Milly gave an angry groan.

But then Monsieur Dufarge, the kindly French teacher, comes in and Sara speaks French to him—explaining that she already knows the language. We all laughed delightedly at Miss Minchin's humiliation.

Just then, Evie looked out the schoolroom window and gasped. "Miss Minchin! Oh, I mean, Miss Jansen! I'm so sorry, you are nothing at all like Miss Minchin! But look outside!"

We all crowded to the window. The air was completely still. Not a flake of snow was falling. But on the horizon was an eerie, purple-yellow color above a rim of blackness. The strangeness of it made a cold shudder run over me.

"What is it?" I asked. "Is more snow coming?"

"That's not just snow," Miss Jansen said. I could tell she was struggling to sound calm. "That's a blizzard coming on. We don't have enough fuel to stay warm in the schoolhouse. School is dismissed. We must get you home. Quick as you can, children. Cover your whole faces except for your eyes."

When we were all bundled up, Miss Jansen divided us into two groups. "Evie, you and Shoshana live just to the north of the school, right? And Milly and Nils, you're to the east. I'm boarding with Milly's family, so I'll go with them."

"What about me?" Irene wailed. "Clive's supposed to fetch me. Do I have to stay here all by myself? What should I do?"

"You go with one of the groups. Clive will realize that's what you've done. And children," Miss Jansen said, "whichever house you get to first, stop there! You can go on to your own homes when the blizzard dies down. If we hurry, we'll all get safely to a house before the blizzard gets too bad. I'll take this lantern," she said, lighting one. "Evie, you take this one. Everyone, hold onto each other. Stay together, whatever you do!"

A powerful blast of wind rattled the schoolhouse windowpanes and moaned in the stovepipe as Miss Jansen extinguished the fire. Evie and I linked arms, and we went out into the howling wind.

Twenty-Nine

The wind, stronger than it had ever been, whipped the breath out of my mouth and yanked my skirts behind me, tight against my legs. I stumbled, tangled in them, and then the wind whipped the other direction, whisking my skirts up and out ahead. Cold air rushed up my legs, making me shudder.

Evie and I stumbled together down the ridge path. Before we had gone even a few feet, a grayish darkness rushed over the sky, like sudden night. Snow started to fall rapidly—tiny, icy pellets that stung my face.

Evie held up the lantern. The pale point of light made the snow around it look as if it were falling in whirling circles. We fought the storm, pushing forward. The wind was like a vast hand pushing us backwards, ripping our hair out of our caps and shawls, yanking it forward and then slashing it across our eyes, blinding us. I concentrated on putting one foot in front of the other. The blizzard seemed to have torn away everything else in the world except me, plodding ahead in a whirl of whiteness. Evie was just an arm linked through mine, a dim white shape to my right.

Soon the path wasn't visible ahead of us. I slowed, and Evie did too, carefully setting one foot directly in front of the other, trying to go in a straight line. I was sure that we were. But suddenly my right foot slipped out from under me, and I fell, gasping as my legs hit the freezing snow. Evie tugged me back upright.

"Too far to the right," I shouted. "We're going downhill!"

Evie nodded, and we struggled blindly back up to what seemed to be the top of the ridge, holding each other tightly to keep from falling. We trudged on into chaotic, swirling whiteness.

Evie shouted something I couldn't hear.

"What?" I shouted back. The cold froze my teeth. Snow blew at my eyes, making me squint. Ice crusted on the muffler over my mouth. I knocked it off with my hand and struggled to pull air into my lungs.

"My house?" Evie shouted in my ear. "Closer? But we'd need to find our way across the field—there's no path."

"No!" I shouted as loudly as the wind would let me. "Mine. We can turn at the stream. And follow it to the house."

Evie shouted something I couldn't hear. She squeezed my arm twice. That seemed to mean yes. I squeezed back. We struggled on and on, pushing through the snow, gasping for breath, trying to keep to the top of the ridge.

Then my right arm jerked downward, and suddenly Evie was gone.

"Evie!" I shouted, flailing my arms around in every direction. In front of me. Behind me. I turned around, screaming. "Evie! Evie Pedersen!"

Nothing.

There was nothing there. How could it have happened? She had vanished. As if she had never been. Where was she? What had happened? I was terrified for her. And then, after a few heartbeats, I realized I was terrified for myself too.

I was alone. Alone and unable to see anything but white. Unable to hear anything but howling wind. Alone in this blank, blinding chaos.

And I could never find my way home now. Turning and calling for Evie, I had lost track of what direction we had been heading. I bent over and squinted at the ground, but without a lantern, I couldn't even see if we had left a trail of footsteps.

I stood still, petrified. What if I moved again and went the wrong way? I could feel if I started going downhill again. But if, by some miracle, I stayed on the flat top of the ridge, how could I know if I was heading in the direction of home or back toward the schoolhouse, where the ridge gradually flattened out and I would be lost forever on the trackless prairie?

I stood, panting through my muffler, staring desperately around me, seeing only whirling whiteness. The cold seemed to seize me and settle deep, deep into my teeth, into my bones.

Then a muffled sound came from down by my feet. A groan. A sound that wasn't the wind.

"Evie?" I squatted and felt around. My mittened hand brushed something, then was caught. A shawl? "Evie!" I screamed.

Suddenly, in the whiteness, I saw a shape that might have been Evie's red hood. And then a hand grabbed mine. It was Evie! She must have fallen into a hollow filled by drifted snow. I took a firm hold of her wrist. "Hang on!" I shouted. I felt around blindly for her other hand, just guessing at where it should be. Another hand grabbed onto me. "I'll pull!" I yelled.

And with all my strength, squatting, pushing upward with my back and legs, I pulled. Evie must have scrabbled for a foothold, because I surely wasn't pulling all of her weight. I heaved and tugged, and then she was up. All of a sudden I saw a flash of light from the lantern, which somehow she was still clinging to, and I fell over backwards and snow was in my eyes and mouth. And then I was up again, and we were hugging, and she shouted something I couldn't hear. She squatted down, flashing the lantern to find our footprints. They were filling in fast, but they were still there. With our arms linked tightly again, we struggled on in the opposite direction from the footprints.

By the time the ridge began to slope down to the stream, I couldn't feel my feet anymore. The blizzard lightened for a moment in the shelter of the ridge, and I saw a silvery, icy streak in the whirling white. We turned, following the bank.

Evie pushed the lantern into my hand. She must be exhausted from holding it.

I stretched my numb arm forward, watching the pale light, following its glitter along the icy stream. My hands trembled.

My belly ached, a hard, cold knot of pain, as if I had swallowed a huge lump of ice. How much longer could we stay alive in this bitter, ferocious, whirling world? I slipped, and Evie pulled me back to my feet. I yanked her toward me and drew my arm all the way through hers, until I felt her body against my side.

Had we gone far enough along the creek? Or too far? If we passed the dugout, we would end up on open prairie. There, even if we were together, we would wander hopelessly until we froze.

Evie was counting on me to lead the way. It was my home we were heading toward.

But in the gray-white darkness, piled with snow, the familiar creek looked different. I bent lower, shining the lantern forward, peering at the creek. Was this the bend where we had paddled on our first washday? Or was that it up ahead?

My head ached. My thoughts came slowly. I could hardly breathe, the icy pellets drove so hard and fast into my face. I could hardly see through my squinted eyes. Wouldn't the clouds ever part, wouldn't the snow let up, even a tiny bit, to give us just a sliver of light so I could find my way? The lantern only flashed a few feet ahead.

And then I saw it. A gleam, a glimmer. Was it an illusion? Or was that home? I had almost passed it. Evie trudged on. I pulled her arm.

"No! Back! This way!"

Leaving the stream behind us, we struggled through trackless white, following the flickering glow. It seemed to be growing stronger. My eyes teared in the wind.

My fist, stretched out ahead with the lantern, bumped into something solid and hard. I switched the lantern to my right hand and felt with my left. Something shaggy and prickly. The frozen grass on a dugout!

I passed the lantern to Evie, and, arms linked, we followed the wall. If the blur of brightness was our dugout window, then this was the way to the door. I felt wood. My hands were too numb to lift a latch, even if I could see it. I thudded with my mittened fists as hard as I could, over and over.

Mama pulled the door open. Light flew out. Mama grabbed me and Evie and pulled us in, to the fire, to my family, to home.

Thirty

My brain felt half-numb. My body too. I seemed to be waking slowly from a bewildering dream. It was so quiet. Why was it so quiet? Then the fire crackled. The bed creaked. The silence I heard was the dugout walls muffling the howling wind. The wind was outside now, and we were inside, safe. Who was I with? My head struggled to remember. Yes, me and Evie. My face prickled and stung. My hands too. Someone breathed next to me, shivering. Cold fabric against me hurt and chafed, then slowly warmed. My feet were tucked against something hard and warm. Warmth rose up my legs, spreading through me.

A brick. Mama had warmed a brick, wrapped it in flannel, and tucked it at our feet. I was in our bed, next to Evie, under mountains of quilts and feather beds. Was Evie all right? I hadn't heard her talk in a long, long time.

I struggled to sit up.

"Shoshana?" It was Libke's voice, gentle, speaking Yiddish. "Mama made you tea with raspberry jam. Can you drink?"

I reached for the glass in its metal holder and held it between my shaking hands, breathing in the steam.

"It'll warm you from the inside. Don't just hold it. Drink, drink!" Mama commanded. "Libke, ask Evie if she's warm enough to sit up and drink tea."

Tsivia popped up on the other side of Evie. "I can have a sip? Raberry tea for me too?" she asked hopefully.

"Not now," said Mama. "Evie and Shoshana were in the cold a long time. They need it first."

Evie pushed herself upright too, her face vague, her hair wildly tousled, and reached for the glass Libke held out to her. "Thank you," she murmured.

I sipped the tea, sweet and fruity and bitter at the same time. It tasted like the long-ago Ukrainian summer. Like plants baking in the sun. Like bees hovering near fallen, overripe fruit. Warmth flowed down my throat and into the icy knot in my belly, slowly loosening it.

Libke sat on the bed and put her arm around me, squeezing me in the old way. "We were so worried! The blizzard came up so suddenly. Papa and Anshel tied a rope to the house and went out with lanterns, swinging around in an arc as far as they could go on the rope, calling for you."

My throat swelled with sudden tears. I leaned closer to her and bent my head over my tea.

When I had blinked my eyes clear, I looked at Libke's worried face. "Papa and Anshel, did they come back?"

"I'm here!" Anshel was standing over me. "Papa's in the barn seeing to the stock. We tied a rope between the house and the barn. Papa will follow it so he doesn't lose his way. I'm just taking a break from shoveling a path."

"I'm ready to get up," I said. I pushed off the covers and stood up, unsteadily. Libke threw a quilt around my shoulders.

Evie got up too. "I'm warm all through now, thank you, Mrs. Rozumny," she said, her voice a little blurry. "The tea really helped."

Mama fussed over us, draping quilts over the crates by the fire and patting other quilts over our shoulders. Zissel leaped onto my lap. I stroked her, feeling her rumbling purr.

"*A dank*, Mama. I'm fine now," I told her drowsily in Yiddish.

Evie looked at me curiously, and I realized she had never heard me speaking Yiddish before. Part of me noticed that, and at the same time another part wondered why it had mattered so much to me. We always spoke Yiddish at home. And she knew my family came from a different country. Of course we spoke a different language. Why had I ever been embarrassed?

Mama and Libke and the twins crowded around us. Anshel sat cross-legged in front of the fire wrapped in a blanket, drinking raspberry jam tea, with Berchik's head on his leg. Berchik looked up at me and thumped his tail against the floor.

"I wish I'd seen this coming," Anshel said in Yiddish. "Papa and I have been through these prairie blizzards before. But this one came up so suddenly, it took everyone by surprise."

I looked at Evie, who was listening quietly to the foreign sounds. "Anshel says, no one knows the blizzard come so fast."

"I know!" Evie nodded her head vigorously. "My parents didn't know it was coming. None of us did at school either! Not even Miss Jansen!"

"How did you two find your way home, *mamele*?" Mama asked, hugging me close and kissing the top of my head. "We couldn't see anything but a wall of whiteness out the window and door."

"We followed the ridge, the way Anshel taught me and Libke," I said. "And then, when it slopes down to the creek, we followed the creek. I did almost walk too far." I shuddered, imagining us still wandering, lost, in icy whiteness.

"How did you find the house?" Mama asked. She smiled at Evie apologetically and tried a little English. "How you and Evie find *duck-out*?"

"A light," I said. "I saw a light in the window."

For the first time, I looked at the small glass pane. On the windowsill stood our menorah. It was the seventh night, so eight little tallow candles flickered in it, one for each night plus the *shames*, reflected against the glass. Sixteen dancing, beckoning candle flames. That was the light that had brought me home.

Thirty-One

Papa came in, looking like a walking snowbank. Mama rushed to help him remove his outer clothes. Chunks of ice fell from his muffler as she unwound it.

"Thank you, Mirele," Papa said, when he was free of his overcoat and hat and muffler. "The wind out there! This is worse than any blizzard we've seen before. It blows so fiercely, it's hard to breathe. Don't go out again until it dies down some, Anshel. The stock are all snug in the barn now, with plenty of hay and water."

Papa hugged me, smelling like snow and sweet hay. "You're all right, my Shoshi? You gave us quite a scare! And you are Evie Pedersen, Frank Pedersen's daughter?" he asked, switching into English. "I'm happy to meet you, but not in this way! I'm so glad you made it here safely."

Evie looked anxiously at the window. "My parents will be worrying dreadfully. I need to get home!"

Papa shook his head and uttered a deep sigh. "Of course. But they'll trust that you took shelter. You'll have to wait until the blizzard is over."

"I'm the wind! Look at me, I'm the wind!" Pearlie called in Yiddish, twirling with her arms out.

"Me too! Whoo-eeeee!" Tsivia and Pearlie spun wildly around the room, making me feel dizzy again.

Evie laughed a little. "Are your little sisters being the storm?" she asked. "I remember when I used to play like that! I used to pretend I was a cat. Shoshana, could I have a turn holding Zissel?"

"Sure." I passed Zissel to her.

Zissel lifted her head, stretched, got to her feet, and settled back down on Evie's lap. Evie beamed. "Zissel likes me, Shoshana!"

"Watch it!" called Anshel, as Pearlie, still twirling, almost hit a bucket standing by the stove with a ladle in it. "Don't knock over the pickle brine!"

I stood up, feeling stiff and achy all over, and looked into the bucket. "That's pickle brine? What are you doing with it, Anshel?"

"Your head's still muddled from the blizzard, I guess!" Anshel said.

"That's not funny," Mama said. "Be kind to your sister. We almost lost her!"

"She knows I'm just teasing! Remember how the pickle brine melted the ice that day? So as soon as the blizzard started, I got a big bucketful from the root cellar. I poured a bit outside the dugout door. It isn't icy there, even now. Didn't you notice when you came in?"

I shook my head, still feeling bone-tired.

"I guess Shoshana had other things on her mind," Libke said softly.

"Sure. Well, when the snow slows, I'm going to pour the brine over the barn path to see if it keeps it clear. I think it will."

"Shoshi spill pickles!" said Pearlie, jumping back onto the bed. "I help!"

We all laughed. Evie turned her face curiously from speaker to speaker. I felt too tired to translate, but she didn't seem to mind. Papa settled down wearily on the bench and gave a big sigh. Mama wrapped a quilt around him and hurriedly poured him a glass of tea with a big spoonful of raspberry jam, adding hot water from the samovar. Papa took the glass between both hands and breathed in its fragrance.

The fire crackled and flickered. Wind sighed in the chimney pipe. I heard a scrape as Mama slid the jam jar back on the shelf. Outside, something banged.

Then I heard a thump nearby, and then a scrabbling noise. Then, loudly and unmistakably, someone thudded, over and over, on our dugout door.

Papa looked up. "Someone's out there!"

Mama rushed to open the door. A man fell in, as tall as Papa. Or at first he looked like a man. Libke hurried to help him off with his hat and muffler, but he shook his head at her.

"My horse!" he gasped. "He can't breathe!"

It was Clive Huber. Right there, in my house. I felt shaky and sick and as if I might throw up. I backed away, hardly noticing what I was doing until I bumped the far wall. And then I realized he was talking about Domino.

"I can't get the ice off Domino's face anymore," Clive wheezed out. "He's nearby, but he won't move. He'll die if I don't! Can I borrow a hammer and chisel?"

Thirty-Two

Domino could die. Domino, with the noble head and gentle brown eyes. Clive Huber was horrible. But I loved Domino more than I hated Clive. I wasn't going to let Domino suffocate out there in the blizzard alone.

I already had my shawl and hood and muffler on. I was pulling on my boots when Mama, who had hurried to fetch the chisel and hammer, noticed.

"What are you doing, Shoshana?" she demanded.

I grabbed the bucket of pickle brine.

"I have to, Mama!" I shouted over my shoulder, and Clive and I plunged out together into the blizzard.

Instantly, we were in another world, a world of numbing, whirling whiteness. It was impossible even to see the door we had just closed. I fumbled blindly for the rope by the door, thrusting my mittened hand into snow, flailing against the hard edge of the doorframe, until I caught the rope, already taut from where Clive was pulling it out ahead of me.

I didn't like letting him take the lead, but he knew where Domino was. Not far, he'd said. I hoped he was right, because I didn't know how long the rope was. And even for Domino, I wouldn't go beyond the end.

Nothing seemed real outside. Everything had disappeared. All that was left was the overwhelming power of the wind. Mightier than people. Mightier than animals. Mightier than the land itself.

Only my eyes were uncovered. Snow struck them mercilessly. I remembered the lacy prettiness of the paper snowflakes we had decorated the schoolhouse with, and inside myself I laughed at how wrong those snowflakes were.

Snow was not like that. Not North Dakota snow.

This snow was tiny, icy, angry, rock-hard pellets.

North Dakota blizzard snow was like Clive Huber and his friends grabbing me in the hollow. Vicious. Merciless.

The wind thrashed the ice pellets into my face, into my uncovered eyes, driving into me where I was most vulnerable.

A blur of red came over my vision. I rubbed my eye and saw a streak of blood on my mitten.

But Domino was out there, his heart beating warmly, desperately, while the storm raged around him. I wouldn't let the blizzard win.

I ducked my head, and stumbled forward.

I was furious at the storm. Furious at Clive. I was out here in this miserable, howling bleakness because Clive had brought that noble horse, a horse he didn't deserve, out into this.

The only thing that was real was the hot rage in the center of my chest, the rope under my mitten, the pail of pickle brine in my other hand, the ache in my lungs.

I bumped into Clive's back and recoiled. Behind him loomed a dark shape. Domino! I saw, through the blur of white, Domino's black sides sucking in and out, in and out, so desperately that his ribs showed each time.

I shoved the bucket of brine into a snowbank to keep it upright.

"Domino! Easy, boy," I crooned, hoping he could somehow hear the vibrations of my voice under the inhuman roar of the wind. I petted his flank, stumbling toward his head.

"Get back, Shoshana!" Clive shouted. He tugged frantically at huge chunks of ice that had formed over Domino's eyes and nostrils. Poor Domino! His warm breath, flowing upwards, had turned to ice. It was blinding and suffocating him. The ice wouldn't budge.

Clive had the chisel and hammer in his hands now. He positioned the chisel against the ice and lifted the hammer.

I couldn't stand it. If Clive's hand slipped, he could cut Domino badly, even blind him.

"No!" I shouted, grabbing for the hammer.

Clive stumbled backwards and nearly fell. Then he was up again, huge and coming at me, the way he had near the gully.

I couldn't help it. I took a step away. He shoved me and I crashed back into the snow. My head cracked against the metal bucket of brine. I scrambled up, gasping. Had the brine spilled?

No. Only a bit had sloshed out, leaving a greenish stain on the snow. I moved toward Domino's head again.

Clive shouted. The wind roared. "Going to die!" I heard. "Have to do it!"

Domino stamped and let out a strange, muffled groan.

"Try this first!" I shouted.

The pickle brine had worked on the ice outside our dugout door. I grabbed for the bucket and ladled out a still-warm scoop of liquid. Gently and carefully, crooning to Domino the whole time, I tipped it so that it ran down the lump of ice clogging his nose.

"What are you doing?" screamed Clive in my ear.

"It softens ice!" I scrabbled frantically at the lump of ice on Domino's nose. A little bit came off. Not much, but more than when Clive had tried just before.

Clive ran to the other side of Domino's head. He rubbed at Domino's nostrils again, and more bits came flying. "More!" he shouted.

I poured another ladleful, crooning to Domino. Clive and I scratched and rubbed. Bit by bit, the ice thinned. After the last ladleful of brine, I reached high on Domino's nose and pulled downward. The whole last chunk slid off. Domino snorted wildly and tossed his head. The last pieces of ice flew off his eyes. He stamped his front hooves and tossed his head again, taking in great gulps of air.

"It worked!" I shouted up into the whirling whiteness.

Clive grabbed Domino's bridle line. "Come on, boy! What is that stuff?"

The wind was slowing. I could hear his voice better. It was like coming up from underwater.

"Pickle brine!" I exulted. "It melts ice!"

All at once, the wind stilled. It was an illusion, surely. A trick. The wind was pretending to let up, but in a moment it would roar again. In the sudden stillness, I pushed my hair out of my face, tucking it under my scarf, and sucked in a deep breath. Clive muttered.

"What?"

"Thanks," Clive blurted into the quiet. "And you know, uh, about that day at the campfire . . . uh, sorry."

That was it? That was all he was going to say? It was something, but it wasn't nearly enough. I still couldn't bear to be anywhere near him. I began slogging my way back through the snow toward the dugout. After a few moments, the wind began to howl around us again, louder and louder.

Anshel loomed up out of the whiteness on another rope, holding a lantern.

"I'll take him back to our barn," he shouted. "Go with Shoshana."

Clive didn't let go of Domino. "No! I'm coming!"

"Wipe his face!" I shouted. "Get the brine off."

I was so tired now I could hardly move. I pulled the heavy rope between both hands and trudged toward the glow in our window. Not far now. I looked over my shoulder.

Domino would be warm in our barn soon, stabled with Royt and Muley and Cantor, the way I had imagined him being. Almost as if he were really mine.

Thirty-Three

When Anshel and Clive came in, Mama wrapped them both in quilts and settled them by the fire.

I got up from my crate and moved away. I'd been so busy fighting the blizzard and tending to Domino that there hadn't been room to think about Clive. But now those terrible memories rushed back into my head.

I watched as Mama drew a brick out of the oven, wrapped it in flannel, and tucked it gently at Clive's feet. Would she do that so kindly, tending to him as if he were her own son, if she knew what Clive had done to me?

Maybe not so kindly. But she would still do it.

Clive and his friends had done a horrible thing to me. But he *had* just muttered that he was sorry. And he loved his horse, even if he shouldn't have taken him out in a blizzard. His apology wasn't enough, of course. It was nowhere near enough. But somehow, I felt a little differently now that I'd helped him rescue Domino. It was very confusing. He did truly love another being besides himself, so there was some good in him. And

Clive was here and he needed us. It would be wrong, indecent even, not to help him.

I suddenly remembered the Rabbi Hillel game I used to play with Libke and Anshel. Hardly realizing I was doing it, I picked up my right foot and tucked it behind my left calf.

"What-is-hateful-to-you-do-not-do-to-your-fellow-man." I moved my lips silently, as quickly as I could. "What-is-hateful-to-you-do-not-do-to-your-fellow . . ." Pearlie jumped up from Evie's lap and grabbed me. I wobbled and put my other foot down.

"What is hateful to you, do not do to your fellow man," Rabbi Hillel had told the taunting fool. "All the rest is commentary." That was the heart of Jewish belief. Papa had told us so, many times.

So of course we would shelter even Clive Huber in a blizzard. He was our fellow man, even if he hadn't acted like it. But did his being our fellow man mean I had to forgive him?

"Shoshana," called Mama. "Pay attention! Our guest needs hot tea! Anshel too. Quick!"

I lifted the teapot off the samovar and poured Clive a glass, adding water. Reluctantly, I stirred in a scant half spoonful of our precious raspberry jam. I handed the glass in its metal holder to Mama. I couldn't bear to go anywhere near Clive. Then I poured another for Anshel, stirred in a big sticky spoonful of jam, and brought it to him. He took it, looked from me to Clive, and then back at me, his eyes questioning. I guess he'd noticed I hadn't brought Clive his tea directly. I looked down, not wanting to meet his eyes.

"Drink," Mama urged Clive in English. "Warm up!"

"He'll drink it if he wants it, Mama," Anshel said, his voice cool. "You don't need to fuss over him."

Clive took a sip of tea. "Thank you!" he said loudly. His voice was raspy and slow. "It's good!"

Mama patted his arm.

Clive was staring at the whitened window, where the last candle flames on the menorah were guttering out.

"Where's Irene?" Clive croaked out, looking at Evie. "She wasn't at the school."

"She went home with Milly and the others. Oh, Clive! You drove out to the school to get her?" Evie put her hand over her mouth.

"Too late," Clive croaked. "Schoolhouse was dark."

That's why Clive had taken Domino out in this? To get his sister? Maybe I should have given him more jam. Not a whole spoonful. But maybe a tiny bit more than I had.

"Got lost. But I had to," he croaked out.

"Miss Jansen told Irene not to stay at the school waiting. Irene left with Milly Hanson and the others, heading to the Hanson farm."

"You'll spend the night here, son," Papa said in English.

Son! I thought. But Papa was seeing a whole new side of Clive, so different from the way he was at school.

Anshel made a low sound in his throat and glanced at me. "Clive can have my pallet," he said. "I'll sleep on some quilts across the room, next to the girls."

I felt an arm go around me. Libke was standing beside me, her face fiercely protective.

I still hadn't told either her or Anshel what had happened with Clive and the others. I would tell them someday. Sometime when it was further behind me.

But Anshel must know, from having gone to school with him, what Clive was like. He'd offered to sleep on the cold earthen floor next to our bed so that I would feel safe. I was sure of that. I wondered what Anshel had seen Clive do at school before.

And somehow, right now, even though I hadn't told her even as much as I had mutely confessed to Anshel that night in the barn, Libke also knew how I was feeling. She knew that I needed her. That I needed my big sister.

Thirty-Four

Four girls in the same bed is a lot. And that night, with Evie staying over while the blizzard blew itself out, we had five.

Usually I wanted more room than I had. Usually, a few times a night, I yanked on the quilt to get a little bit more of it or shoved one of my sisters away.

But that night I didn't feel like doing either of those things.

The twins were squashed up against Evie, fast asleep. Pearlie's back was against me, and Libke was on my other side. On top of me, the quilt and the feather bed moved up and down as my sisters breathed. Tsivia murmured in her sleep. Without saying anything, Libke reached for my hand. And she fell asleep holding it.

When I woke in the night, hearing the wind howling and moaning outside, Libke still had my hand loosely in hers. Pearlie, squeezed next to me on the other side, was on top of my other arm. I tried to let go of Libke for just a moment to push an itchy piece of hair away from my face.

Libke's hand tightened. Clenched almost. She wasn't even awake, but she didn't want to let me go.

So I just blew the hair off my forehead.

I lay there, listening to the wind roaring outside and the breathing inside. Feeling my big sister's hand warm around mine.

Libke had been so angry with me. She had burned that paper snowflake in the schoolroom stove for no reason.

At least I hadn't thought there was a reason.

She had slapped me.

She had walked off with Nils, leaving me behind.

And even when I had called to her the next morning, even when I had said, "Please Libke, please. Please come back and walk with me," and she should have known how scared I was— shouldn't she?—just from the shaky sound of my voice, just because I never asked her for things like that, and because that morning I *was* asking her, still she wouldn't come back for me.

I had had to run past that place near the gully all alone. That place where those boys had grabbed at me as if I didn't belong to myself. Where they had made me feel like dirt. Worse than dirt, because the prairie was made of dirt, and the prairie was beautiful.

Where they had made me feel like nothing.

But it wasn't my fault.

I couldn't be dirty because of something that Clive and Mac and Fred had done. What they had done showed something about them, not about me. And now that at least Clive had muttered that he was sorry, even though it was too little, even though

I still thought he was awful, maybe I could let the whole thing go. It could all be over for me.

And if Libke had been angry with me, it wasn't because she didn't love me, the way I had thought on all those gray, lonesome days.

Libke's hand, clutching me even while she was asleep, told me that. More than anything she could have said when she was awake.

"Being ashamed of your people is like being ashamed of yourself." That's what Libke had said to me that day in the schoolhouse, almost crying.

"Honor your father and mother, remember? They have loved us, cared for us, worked for us, night and day."

I had thought Libke was just being all goody-goody. Saying she was better than me.

But that wasn't what she meant. She was saying, *Don't be ashamed of who your people are. Don't be ashamed of who you are. No matter what anybody does. No matter what anybody says.*

I should be proud! Proud to come from a people so courageous that they could leave everything behind and make a new beginning in this strange, new place. Proud of how hard we all worked, farming the land, tending to the animals, always treating them with kindness, the way the Torah said, even the smelly chickens, learning a whole new language and new ways in a new country. Sheltering and tending to Evie, and even Clive—who had treated me so badly—when they needed us. Being generous. Being strong.

Yes, we were Jews! Yes, we were different. We weren't like the others. But that didn't make us bad. There was nothing wrong with us being exactly who we were. Being Jews, being us, was something to be proud of.

We didn't have to hide it. We couldn't, anyway.

We didn't have to try to change. To fit in.

What Libke had been saying was that she liked me just exactly the way I was.

And Libke didn't just sort-of like me because we were sisters and sisters have to like each other. What Libke's hand was saying to me, clutching me even while she was asleep, was that she *loved* me, just exactly the way I was.

Me, Shoshana.

Me.

The blizzard lasted all the next day. Evie couldn't go home. Neither, unfortunately, could Clive Huber. And Domino, noble Domino with the gentle brown eyes, a horse so much better and nobler than Clive Huber deserved, was safe and warm in our barn, contentedly munching hay. I visited him each time I pushed my way along the rope through the blizzard to milk Royt.

Night came early, darkening the sky while the wind howled. Anshel came back from the barn with a bundle full of the last Chanukah candles, stamping snow off his feet.

Libke looked at me. I knew what that look meant as clearly as if she had said it out loud. It meant, Are you going to try to hide what we're doing?

But how could you hide anything in a one-room dugout? And last night, I'd decided I didn't want to hide anything anymore anyway.

"I'll put those in the menorah," I said shakily in Yiddish. Anshel handed them to me.

Evie watched me gently push the candles in.

"That's so pretty!" Evie said. "So you do have Christmas decorations! I didn't think you would. You know, because you're Jews and all."

Clive looked over. I felt myself flush.

"The candles aren't for Christmas. Tonight is Chanukah," I said stiffly. "A Jewish holiday."

"What's Chanukah?" Evie asked.

This was going to be hard to explain in English. And with Clive there. I took a deep breath. "Long ago. The Greeks wanted the Jews to be like them," I started. "Not to be Jews. The Greeks took over the Jewish temple. Jews say no, we want to stay Jews! The Jews fight! They win the temple back."

I glanced at Clive, sitting on a crate. "This little Yid's a fighter!" he had mocked me. He blushed, ducking his head. I could see he remembered too. And was at least a little bit ashamed.

Libke was listening also, while grating potatoes.

"But the light in the temple must always burn," I said to Evie, with an intensity that surprised me. "And not enough oil!

But then . . . a miracle! Somehow oil burns for eight days until the Jews get more. So now Jews light eight candles, one more each night, to remember."

"I like that," Evie said softly.

"Can I light the candles tonight, Mama?" I called in Yiddish. "I haven't done it yet."

"Yes. When Papa comes in."

"Be careful not to burn yourself," said Libke. "Keep your hair and your sleeves back. And don't knock it over!"

"I know, Libke!" I protested.

Libke blushed. "Sorry! It's just that it's hard, when there are so many candles so close together."

"And if there's an accident waiting to happen, we all know Shoshi will make it happen!" Anshel teased. But we were all talking Yiddish. Clive couldn't understand and mock me about it later. And Anshel was grinning.

Anshel was only teasing. In the three long years Anshel and Papa had been here without us, I had forgotten how to deal with Anshel's teasing. But by now I knew how. I grinned back.

"I notice Mama never asks you to light them at all, Anshel," I said in Yiddish. "I wonder why that is. Mama knows how to keep accidents from happening!"

Anshel laughed, while Mama protested.

Papa came in, knocking the snow off his boots. When he'd warmed himself, my family gathered at the window. Anshel and Libke stood on either side of me. Mama and Papa and the little ones were opposite. Tsivia snuggled against Mama's side with her thumb in her mouth. Pearlie stood on tiptoe, then jumped, trying to be taller. Zissel rubbed against my ankle.

I glanced at Libke. She rested her hand on my shoulder.

Clive stayed where he was by the fire. Evie sat on a blanket, stroking Berchik, watching curiously as we sang the blessing.

My hand wobbled a little as I touched the *shames* to each of the little tallow candles. The wicks caught, one by one. Their tiny lights reflected, dancing in the windowpane, lighting up the still-swirling snow outside.

I imagined each flame sending its light out onto the vast prairie, this place where, before us, no one had ever lit a menorah before. Each light seemed so fragile, as if the slightest wind would blow it out. And the winds here in North Dakota were ferocious.

But the lights of the menorah, all together on this last night of the holiday, burned strong. They stood for the way the Jews carried on.

For the way, wherever we went, we held onto who we were.

Thirty-Five

When I woke up the next morning, something seemed strange. Not Evie curled in our bed. Not the sounds of my sisters breathing. Not Pearlie's foot on top of me.

It was the quiet. And then I realized that the winds that had been howling, moaning, and shrieking for most of the last two days had gone still.

I sat up. Blue glimmered through the windowpane, beyond the remains of last night's candles.

Mama smiled. "Rise and shine! The blizzard is over!"

Snow had mounded in front of the door, blocking it. So I moved the menorah to the table, and Anshel and I climbed out the window to shovel from the outside. It was bitterly cold, but the wind had quieted. The sun blazed blindingly on the snow, bringing out glints of color. When we'd uncovered the front door, Anshel and Clive and Papa shoveled a track to the barn. Not long after, Clive rode off on Domino. Papa said he would walk Evie back to the Pedersen farm.

"Evie, do you think we have school tomorrow?" I asked, going outside with her.

"Sure! The blizzard's over. Today, everybody'll be too busy digging out. But tomorrow night's the Christmas concert! Unless there's another blizzard, which it sure doesn't look like, with all this sun, tomorrow we'll have school and the concert, both. Two years ago we had a storm the day before, and we had the concert anyway. Miss Jansen said, 'The show must go on!' That's her motto!"

I watched Papa and Evie make their way off, pushing slowly through the snow. Before I could lose my nerve, I ran back into the dugout.

"Mama," I panted, pulling off my boots. "Tomorrow night, at school, there's a concert. Will you and Papa come? And everybody? Libke and I learned poems." I'd just had an idea of something I might do instead of reciting the poem, but I wasn't sure about it yet.

Mama turned from the table, wiping her hands on her apron, and looked at me and Libke searchingly.

"A concert!" Mama said, astonished. "Tomorrow night!" I felt my cheeks getting hot. She must know that we'd been getting ready for it for weeks. "Yes, daughters," Mama said slowly. "We will come."

After school the next day, Libke and I filled the tin tub with snow and melted it on the stove so we could have a bath. It felt strange to bathe in the middle of the week.

"I'm so clean!" I told Libke, as we combed out each other's hair. "Two baths in one week! It feels so good."

"I want special bath!" Tsivia said.

"Not now," Mama said, placing the flat iron on the stove to heat. "You're clean enough, little one. This is a special day for your big sisters."

"I wish Zissel and Berchik could come," I said, as Libke worked all the tangles out of my hair.

"And Royt and the oxen?" Libke teased me. "There isn't enough room in the schoolhouse!"

Libke took down her dress, which Mama had hung, damp and steaming, in front of the stove. She pressed her dress carefully, and then I did mine.

"Put the iron back on the stove, Shoshi," Libke said. "I still need to press my ribbon."

She tested the temperature, let the flat iron cool a bit, then gently smoothed the dark-blue ribbon Evie had given her. I helped her fasten it around her throat.

Mama was watching. "Very pretty! Would you like to wear your hair up tonight, Libke?" she asked. "You're old enough now."

"Oh, yes, Mama!"

I watched as Mama brushed out Libke's gleaming, wheat-colored hair, and carefully twisted and pinned it up. It framed her delicate face in gold. Her cheeks went pink and her eyes shone as she looked into the little hand mirror nailed to the wall.

"Libke pretty like a butterfly!" breathed Tsivia.

"Libke is pretty like a cat!" shouted Pearlie. "Pretty like . . . a rainbow!"

"And now you, my Shoshana. You don't have a ribbon, I know. You're too young to have your hair up, but you need something special too."

"Shoshana wear *my* ribbon!" Pearlie climbed onto a bench and grabbed her bedraggled green one off the shelf.

"Actually, I have something extra-special for Shoshana to wear tonight. Something I used to wear myself when I was a girl."

Mama knelt by the trunk in the corner and pulled out the small, black enamel box she kept her ornaments in. She handed me something wrapped in a handkerchief.

"My Papa, your Zayde, made this, may his memory be for a blessing. It will look beautiful with your hazel eyes and dark curls."

I opened the handkerchief with my sisters all crowding around me. Inside was a carved wooden brooch, ornately painted, with a black-and-golden border around a cluster of red, pink, and white flowers. The lamplight gleamed off its polished surface.

"It's wonderful!" I said.

Libke looked worried. "It's so special, Shoshi! Don't lose it!" she said, and then she blushed. "I'm sorry. I know you won't!"

Mama smiled and pinned it at my throat, in the center of my freshly ironed gray dress. "Shoshana is older now and more careful," she told Libke.

Pearlie ran over and squeezed my hand. "Shoshana is pretty like a cat now too," she said earnestly.

After a quick, early supper, Mama and Papa dressed carefully for the recital. I watched as Mama got her next-best *shtern-tikhl* out of the bundle under her side of the bed. It was lovely, a silvery gray with pale blue and yellow and green glints in it. But it would still make her look so different from the other mothers.

I tried not to say it. I almost didn't say it. But then the words came bursting out. "Are you sure you want to wear that tonight, Mama? Other women here don't wear them. Instead, you could put your hair up fancy like Libke's."

Libke frowned at me.

"I feel more comfortable in my *shtern-tikhl* outside the house," Mama said quietly but firmly. "It's our tradition. Help me tie it on, won't you, Shoshi?"

I helped her tuck and pin, feeling the soft fabric under my fingers. She smiled at me, her eyes warm, her face strong, under the cloth.

We heard the jingling of the Pedersens' sleigh approaching and pulled on our boots. I had made up my mind. I whispered something to Papa. He nodded, hung back as the rest of us hurried out through the bitter cold, then came out with something wrapped in a blanket. We all cuddled together with Evie and Frances on the two seats, facing each other under a thick pile of buffalo robes.

"Off we go!" called Mr. Pedersen cheerfully, flicking the reins. The ride was as wonderful as I'd thought a ride in a sleigh would be, swift and smooth over the packed white snow, the jingle of the bells musical in the cold stillness, the stars high and bright overhead.

The schoolhouse was crowded and blazing with light. Miss Jansen, elegant in a brown silk dress, lined up the performers beside the teacher's platform.

"Welcome to our Christmas concert," she said, when everyone was in place. "Our scholars have worked hard preparing their pieces and decorating the schoolhouse."

I noticed Mama and Papa looking around at the snowflakes and Christmas card cutouts on the walls. The lady to Mama's right glanced at her, and I saw her eyes rove over Mama's headscarf. Heat prickled on my cheeks. In the back of the schoolhouse, Clive Huber lounged, his arms crossed, his face set, next to his mother and surly Mr. Huber. But at least he wasn't staring and jeering at my parents.

Miss Jansen beckoned to the smallest children, little Emily and Betsy and Lars. They trooped up onto the platform, looking very small and sweet. When she gestured to them, they began to sing: "O, Christmas tree, O, Christmas tree."

They looked like little angels. It didn't even matter when Betsy started to pick her nose, and Emily reached over to yank her hand down. A ripple of laughter ran through the audience. When the song ended, the parents applauded warmly. Lars bowed five times, until Miss Jansen took his hand and led him offstage.

Then Milly, Evie, Irene, and Grace, holding a cloth doll rolled up in a blanket, took their places onstage. Irene stood in the middle of the back row and Grace settled on her knees in front, gazing down at the doll as they sang "Silent Night." I had to admit that they probably sounded better without my voice, which did sometimes have trouble following a tune.

Nils and Libke and I stood at the side of the platform, waiting.

Beside me, Libke was twisting the fabric of her sleeve nervously. Nils stepped closer to her. "I know it's hard before you speak the first time in English in front of everybody," he said softly. "I remember. But as soon as you say the first words, the rest comes easy."

"Now, we have two new scholars, Libke and Shoshana, who came to America just two months ago," Miss Jansen announced. "They will show how much they have learned by reciting short poems in English. First, Libke will recite together with Nils Andersson."

Libke looked panicked. *"We are but minutes,"* I whispered to her. "You can do it."

Side by side, Nils and Libke walked onto the stage. I saw his fingers brush against hers. Did he think no one would see? I was pretty sure he had done that on purpose.

"We are but minutes, little things," Nils and Libke began. Libke's voice faltered at first, but then she held up her head and spoke strongly, all the way through the verses.

The audience applauded. Nils and Libke smiled at each other. Mama and Papa beamed.

And then it was my turn. Miss Jansen beckoned me forward.

I stood in the middle of the teacher's platform all alone, with all those eyes on me. The schoolroom had never seemed so big. Betsy, sitting now in her mother's lap on the front bench, waved. I felt better.

"I was going to recite the poem 'Sunset,'" I said. "Because I love Nordakota sunsets." I bit my lip, embarrassed at my slip. "North Dakota. I love North Dakota sunsets," I corrected myself. "But I change my mind. I want to play a piece on my Papa's fiddle instead. This is all right, Miss Jansen?"

Miss Jansen smiled her agreement, and Papa came forward, handing me the fiddle case. I set it down, opened it, and drew out the beautiful, honey-colored fiddle. I took a deep breath.

"Libke," I called in Yiddish, right in front of everyone, "Come up and sing with me?"

Libke, her cheeks rosy in the lamplight, climbed back onto the stage. She gave me a wondering look.

I turned to the audience and spoke in English. "The song is in Yiddish, our language. Its name is '*Oyfn Pripetshik.*' It's about children learning letters. It's about beginnings."

I put the fiddle to my shoulder, and tuned it.

Would I be clumsy in my nervousness? Would the bow screech? Would my audience get up and leave, howling like Berchik?

Anshel sat on the bench next to Papa and Mama. Tsivia snuggled against Mama. Pearlie wriggled on Anshel's lap. She put bent fingers up to her head, and I saw she was making cat ears, reminding me of Zissel, who couldn't come with us. Zissel never left the room when I played. Anshel grinned at me, pretending to gasp and cover his ears. His teasing gave me confidence. I looked at Libke. I drew the bow down, sweet and true.

Libke sang. "*Oyfn pripetshik brent a fayerl / Un in shtub iz heys . . .*" "On the hearth a fire burns / And the house is warm . . ." My fiddle notes and Libke's pure voice blended as if they were meant to be together, always. The way sisters are.

"Fiddle like bird." That was what Pearlie had said when she had first heard Papa play. I felt myself lift and fly with the song. I saw the silver birches of Liubashevka, whitened by moonlight. I smelled apples ripening on the trees. I saw Mama's fingers, because she wasn't always so busy and tired there, embroidering by lamplight. Ducks passing on the river under the willows, so serene above the water, but if you looked closely you could see their little webbed feet paddling madly underneath. The smoke rising from the chimney of our cottage in winter.

But I also felt the beauty around me here. The undulating stretches of the prairie. The flaming sunsets. The vast, free space to run. The sweet smell of dried grasses. The exhilarating power of the wind. The unending sky. The raucous, free cry of the cranes. The beaded bird, so surprising, so vivid, on Nani's bag. Zissel bounding to meet me through the grass. Berchik resting by the fire, his head on Anshel's lap. Evie's freckled, smiling face.

Like the migrating sandhill cranes, the ones I loved, the ones Nani loved maybe even more, because it had been her prairie first, I came from far. I might not be here to stay. But our

Yiddish music, the rich sounds of the fiddle filling this North Dakota schoolhouse, reaching out into the dark prairie around us, like the cry of the cranes, this was the song of where I came from and of where I was going. It was the song of who I was. It was my music of the journey.

Yeder onheyb iz shver. All beginnings were difficult, the way the song said.

This North Dakota beginning, making a living on this hard land where not everyone wanted us, this beginning was difficult, no doubt about it.

But life stretched out before us, as wide open as the North Dakota prairie.

Beginnings were beautiful too.

If you held onto who you were.

If you played your own music.

If you kept your own light burning.

Author's Note

Shoshana and her family leave their small village, Liubashevka in Ukraine, then part of the Russian Empire, because of pogroms—systematic, violent attacks on Jewish homes, businesses, and people. The police and the military made no attempt to stop pogroms, and, in fact, the pogroms were encouraged by the tsarist government. Sometimes the violent attacks were spearheaded by local civic and church authorities.

Jews in the Russian Empire were also subject to many harsh laws. Laws expelled Jews from cities and villages, forced them to live in the restricted territory of the Pale of Settlement, limited their movement, and allowed young Jewish boys to be forced into the tsar's army for twenty-five years. Other laws imposed strict limits on education for Jews and restricted their occupations. From the 1870s to the 1920s, because of this persecution, two and a half million Eastern European Jews fled the lands ruled by the Russian Empire (including Ukraine, Poland, Latvia, and Lithuania) and immigrated to America.

Most of the Jewish immigrants settled in cities. But a small number, like Shoshana's family, took advantage of the Homestead Act of 1862 and filed for land claims on the prairie, mostly in what became North and South Dakota. The Jews were relative latecomers to homesteading. By the time they arrived, much of the best farming land had already been claimed by others, leaving them to struggle with poor soil and a dry climate as well as other challenges of homesteading, such as grasshoppers, prairie fires, and blizzards. Sometimes, in America too, Jews faced antisemitic hostility.

The land was not empty before the settlers arrived. Native Americans lived there. Where Shoshana and her family settle (as well as in South Dakota, Minnesota, and parts of Nebraska and Canada), the previous inhabitants were the Dakota people. The United States government coerced the Dakota into agreeing to treaties, taking vast swaths of land in exchange for money and goods. But the government did not live up to its agreement, and full payment was never made. The Dakota people, forced onto reservation land, unable to access hunting and fishing grounds, were starving. Retaliation by some desperate Dakota warriors led to the US-Dakota War of 1862 and many deaths. Afterwards, many Dakota, including elders, women, and children, were imprisoned in concentration camps, where they died of starvation, cold, and epidemic disease. By the time Shoshana and her family arrive in North Dakota, about fifty years later, a remnant of the surviving

Dakota people were living on reservation land, dispossessed from the land where Native Americans had lived for many generations.

The beadwork Shoshana sees on Nani's bag is a traditional art form of many Native American tribes. Geometric forms are traditional, as are plant and animal forms.

Readers can learn more at the links below.

Learn about the Dakota people:
www.mnhs.org/fortsnelling/learn/native-americans/dakota-people

Learn about the US–Dakota War of 1862:
www.usdakotawar.org

Learn about the history of Jews in the Russian Empire:
www.jewishvirtuallibrary.org/the-pale-of-settlement

I consulted many works of scholarly history, firsthand written accounts, and oral histories in the course of writing this novel. Some of the most helpful are listed below. I am also deeply grateful to Kimimilasha James (Aquinnah Wampanoag and Oglala Lakota) and to Stacey Parshall Jensen (Mandan and Hidatsa) for their meticulous and helpful suggestions about this manuscript.

In spelling personal names and holidays, in a few cases I have deviated slightly from the YIVO method of transliterating Yiddish in order to make them more accessible to English-speaking child readers.

Works Consulted

Bender, Rebecca E. and Kenneth M. *Still*. Fargo: North Dakota State University Press, 2019.

Brooks, Fanny. As told by daughter Eveline Auerbach. *Stories Untold: Jewish Pioneer Women 1850–1910*. www.storiesuntold.org /women/fanny_brooks.html (electronic text).

Calof, Rachel. Edited by J. Sanford Rikoon. *Rachel Calof's Story: Jewish Homesteader on the Northern Plains*. Bloomington: Indiana University Press, 1995.

Clemmons, Linda M. *Dakota in Exile: The Untold Stories of Captives in the Aftermath of the U.S.–Dakota War*. Iowa City: University of Iowa Press, 2019.

Fraser, Caroline. *Prairie Fires: The American Dreams of Laura Ingalls Wilder*. New York: Henry Holt, 2017.

Hansen, Karen V. *Encounters on the Great Plains: Scandinavian Settlers and the Dispossession of Dakota Indians, 1890–1930.* Oxford, UK: Oxford University Press, 2013.

Harris, Lloyd David. *Sod Jerusalems: Jewish Agricultural Communities in Frontier Kansas.* Contributed by Gertrude Harris. Kansas Collection Books. www.kancoll.org/books/harris/sodcontents.htm#introduction (electronic text).

Libo, Kenneth, and Irving Howe. *We Lived There Too: Pioneer Jews and the Westward Movement of America 1630–1930.* New York: St. Martin's Press, 1984.

Lindgren, H. Elaine. *Land in Her Own Name: Women as Homesteaders in North Dakota.* Norman: University of Oklahoma Press, 1996.

Mayer, Rebecca. Memoir of her 1852 honeymoon along the Santa Fe Trail and El Camino Real. Edited by Joy Poole. www.nps.gov/safe/learn/historyculture/trailwide-research.htm (electronic text).

North Dakota Oral History Project. Oral histories housed at North Dakota Historical Society, Bismarck, North Dakota.

Pexa, Christopher J. "Transgressive Adoptions: Dakota Prisoners' Resistances to State Domination Following the 1862 U.S.–Dakota War," *Wicazo Sa Review* 30, no. 1 (Spring 2015), pp.29–56.

Rabin, Shari. *Jews on the Frontier: Religion and Mobility in Nineteenth-Century America*. New York: New York University Press, 2017.

Rochlin, Harriet and Fred. *Pioneer Jews: A New Life in the Far West*. Boston: Houghton Mifflin, 2000.

Schloff, Linda Mack. *"And Prairie Dogs Weren't Kosher": Jewish Women in the Upper Midwest Since 1855*. St. Paul: Minnesota Historical Society Press, 1996.

Sharlip, Fanny Jaffe. Memoir. Jewish Women's Archive. jwa.org/westernpioneers/sharlip-fanny-jaffe (electronic text).

Solomon, Anna Freudenthal. Memoir. Jewish Women's Archive. jwa.org/westernpioneers/solomon-anna-f (electronic text).

Spiegelberg, Flora Langerman. Memoir. Jewish Women's Archive. jwa.org/westernpioneers/spiegelberg-flora-langerman (electronic text).

Thal, Sarah. Edited by Martha Thal. "Early Days: The Story of Sarah Thal 1880–1900." *Western States Jewish History* 39 no. 1 (Fall 2006), 74–85 (electronic text).

Trupin, Sophie. *Dakota Diaspora: Memoirs of a Jewish Home-steader*. Lincoln: University of Nebraska Press, 1984.

Acknowledgments

I am deeply grateful to Patti Gauch and Gary D. Schmidt for their inspirational master classes at the Highlights Foundation and at Whale Rock Workshops, as well as to Shari Becker for the tireless, behind-the-scenes work that made the latter possible. You have made me a better, freer, and happier writer. Jaya Mehta, my daily writing and critique partner, has been with this book almost every step of the way, helping me shape this novel in countless and invaluable ways. Thank you also to the writers in my critique groups—Patty Bovie, Susan Lubner, Anna Staniszewski, Jane Kohuth, Sarah Lamstein, and Terry Farish—for your friendship, encouragement, and advice over many years. I am grateful to my mother, Marilyn Pettit, for telling me a story of her kitten escaping in a train station restroom with pay toilets, a story that made its way into this book!

Kimimilasha James (Aquinnah Wampanoag and Oglala Lakota) and Stacey Parshall Jensen (Mandan and Hidatsa) read this novel in manuscript and offered expert commentary and guidance, for which I am very grateful. Your suggestions improved and enriched this book. Julia Litsina and Ella Mints enthusiastically helped me with translations of Ukrainian and information about Ukraine. My Wellesley English Department colleagues, and particularly Cord Whitaker, helped me brainstorm about titles and deepen the idea of "song." Cappy Lynch and Alison Hickey helped me with some matters of wording. I am grateful to Solon Beinfeld, Harry Bochner, and Miriam Udel for generously helping me with their expert knowledge of Yiddish, and to Larry Rosenwald for introducing me to Solon and Harry. Rabbi Dena Bodian generously answered obscure questions about animal fat and candle-making. Kenneth Winkler, my go-to expert on all ornithological matters, shared with me his knowledge of sandhill cranes.

A sabbatical leave from Wellesley College gave me time to think, research, and write. In the early stages of the writing of this book, I was fortunate enough to be selected as a writer-in-residence at Hedgebrook, where I enjoyed space and time to create as well as the companionship of other women writers, an enchanting cottage, and home-grown organic meals. PJ Our Way supported this novel with a much-appreciated Author Incentive Manuscript Award. I am also grateful to the Willa Cather Foundation, as it was when I was participating in their conferences and seminars that I first spent time on the Great Plains. Willa Cather's depictions of the beauty of the prairie lie behind mine. Very attentive readers may also notice a moment of homage to Emerson.

My heartfelt thanks go to my agent, Rena Rossner, for championing my work. Rena gave practical advice, offered insightful criticism, and brought my novel to the attention of the perfect editor. I am grateful to Laura Schreiber, my editor at Union Square Kids, for loving my characters and my story and for the astute editorial guidance that has made this a better novel.

My large extended family, especially Nadine Meyer, Alison Meyer, Nick Meyer, Steven Meyer, David Meyer, Christina Qian, Becky Winkler, and Madeline Winkler, gave me much-appreciated companionship and moral support during the writing of this book.

My husband, Kenneth Winkler, enabled me to keep going through painful adversity. This book is dedicated to you.